DEADLY LITTLE LIES

A TOUCH NOVEL

Laurie Faria Stolarz

HYPERION

NEW YORK

Also by Laurie Faria Stolarz

Copyright © 2009 by Laurie Faria Stolarz
All rights reserved. Published by Hyperion, an imprint of Disney Book Group.
No part of this book may be reproduced or transmitted in any form or by any means, electronic or mechanical, including photocopying, recording, or by any information storage and retrieval system, without written permission from the publisher.
For information address Hyperion, 114 Fifth Avenue,
New York, New York 10011-5690.
First Hyperion paperback edition
3 5 7 9 10 8 6 4 2
V475-2873-0-13207
Printed in the United States of America
Library of Congress Cataloging-in-Publication Data on file.
ISBN 978-1-4231-1199-3
Visit www.hyperionteens.com

SUSTAINABLE FORESTRY INITIATIVE

Certified Chain of Custody
Promoting Sustainable Forestry
www.sfiprogram.org
SFI-01054
The SFI label applies to the text stock

For Ed, Ryan, and Shawn
with love and gratitude

DEADLY LITTLE LIES

I

I'VE BEEN HAVING TROUBLE SLEEPING. Most nights, I find myself lying awake in bed, unable to nod off.

And unable to take my mind off him.

The strength of his hands.

The way he smelled—a mix of sugar and sweat.

And the branchlike scar that snaked up his arm.

Ever since Ben left four months ago, I've been getting fixated on these little things, trying to remember if his scar had three branches or four, if it was his left or his right thumb knuckle that always looked a little swollen, and if his sugary smell was more like powdered doughnuts or cotton candy.

Sometimes I think I'm going crazy. And I'm not just saying that to be dramatic. I really question my sanity. Things just haven't been right lately. *I* haven't been right.

And I guess that's what scares me the most.

Like last night. Once again unable to sleep, I crept into the hallway and down to the basement. My dad, who firmly believes that we all should have our own personal work space, has designated the area behind his tool bench as my pottery studio. And so I have a wheel, bins full of carving tools, and boxes of clay just waiting to be sculpted.

Wearing a nightshirt and slippers, I decided to work in the dark, inspired by the moon as it poured in through the window, slicing a long strip of light across my table. I cut myself a thick hunk of clay and began to knead it out. With my eyes closed I could feel the moonlight tugging at the ends of my hair, shining over my skin, and swallowing my hands whole.

Keeping focused on the clammy texture of the clay and not what I was actually forming, I tried to relax—to stop the whirring inside my mind.

But then it hit me. The image of Ben's scar popped into my head. And so I started sculpting it—feeding this weird, insatiable need inside me to form his arm, from his fingertips to just past his elbow. My fingers worked fast, as if independent of my mind—as if they knew exactly the way things should be, while my brain just couldn't keep up.

At least thirty minutes later, long after my fingers had turned waterlogged, I took a step back to take it all in— what I had sculpted and what it could possibly mean. Sitting on my worktable was my sculpture of Ben's arm— his scar, the muscles in his wrist, and the bones in his hands.

It was exactly the way it should be—exactly the way I remembered it.

His scar had three branches, not four.

It was his left thumb that looked a little bit swollen, not the right.

The answers to my obsessive little thoughts were right there. I'd sculpted them all out, which absolutely baffled me.

And that's when I heard him: "Camelia," he whispered. His voice sounded just like I'd remembered—soft, smooth, deep, able to steal my breath and make my heart pound.

I turned to look. But, aside from the lingering glow of the moonlight, there was just darkness behind me. A cold, dank basement with cement floors, boxes piled high, and old bicycles parked against the wall. Still, I strained my eyes, wondering if he was there somehow. Maybe he'd snuck in through the garage. Could my mom have forgotten to lock it again?

"Ben?" I whispered into the darkness. I wiped my hands and took a couple steps, but I didn't see anything. An anxious sensation formed in the pit of my stomach.

I reluctantly turned back to my work.

And then I heard it again: "Camelia," he whispered, only louder this time.

My hands shaking, I grabbed a carving knife, just in case, and then switched on the overhead light. Two of the three bulbs blew. A bright bolt of light flashed and then everything went dark.

I moved back, toward the cement wall, hoping for stability, noticing a sudden scraping sound. It was coming from just behind me. I turned to look, realizing I'd bumped a can of paint. It toppled to the floor. Paint spilled out in a creamy dark fluid that reminded me of blood.

I let out a breath and headed toward the back of the basement, past our collection of ski equipment and gardening shovels, knowing that he must be here somewhere.

Watching me.

"Ben?" I called, focused on the stack of boxes in the corner. My insides stirring, I moved closer, accidentally tripping over an old bicycle pump. A yelp sputtered from my throat. The furnace kicked on with a roar, sending a chill straight up my spine.

I peered over my shoulder, wondering if my parents had heard me, if they might come downstairs.

"Is that you?" I whispered, feeling my pulse race.

When no one moved and nothing happened, I pushed the stack of boxes so that they toppled to the ground. Old clothes spilled onto the floor.

"Camelia," he whispered.

It was coming from the top of the stairs now.

I gripped the knife and moved in that direction, following his voice as it led me through the dark kitchen, down an even darker hallway, and then into my bedroom.

I clicked on the light—it stung my eyes—and peered around the room. I checked inside my closet and underneath my bed. But there was no sign of him.

"Ben?" I whispered, wondering if he'd snuck out the window.

I dropped the knife, unlocked the pane, and opened the window wide. The cold January air bit at my skin.

Finally I saw him. He was standing across the street, shrouded by a clump of barren trees in front of my neighbor's house, staring back in my direction.

My head still spinning, I managed to wave. With my other hand I pinched myself, wondering if in only a few moments I would wake up.

But it wasn't a dream. It was real. He was there. The clock on my bedside table read 2:49 a.m.

I waved again, but he didn't wave back. So I grabbed my phone and dialed his cell. It barely even rang before I heard him pick up.

"Ben?" I asked, when he didn't say hello. I looked again out the window, hoping to see him with his phone.

But the figure was no longer there. A second later, the phone clicked off. And when I called back, it went straight to his voice mail.

2

January 22, 1984

Dear Diary,

Today I turned 13 and my sister Jilly gave me you, Diary, as my present. She wrapped you up in a pretty acrylic painting she made of a vase full of roses with swirly stems.

Jilly swore me to secrecy, saying that if I ever told our mother where I got you, she'd never speak to me again.

Because my mother doesn't want me to have presents. Because my mother doesn't want me period.

I promised Jilly I'd do whatever she says. I want her to like me. I want more

surprise gifts like you in the future. And
I also want someone to give them to.

Instead of a cake, I grabbed one of
my sketches, erased most of the angry
scribbles, and then blew the eraser dust
into the air as I made a wish.

I wished for my world to be as pretty as
a vase full of roses with swirly stems.

I wished that I didn't hate myself all
the time.

Love,
Alexia

3

"*W*AIT. *WHAT?*" Kimmie blurts. She sets her latte down on the table with a smack. Her pale blue eyes, framed by a pair of vintage tortoiseshell glasses, widen in disbelief.

It's Sunday—the last night of winter vacation—and she, Wes, and I are sitting at the Press & Grind, the coffee shop downtown, indulging in an array of over-the-counter stimulants in the form of caffeine and chocolate.

"It's true," I say. "I don't know how it happened."

"Okay, so let me get this straight," Wes begins. "It was two a.m., you couldn't sleep, your mind was racing with all kinds of crazy . . . Might you have been smoking something funky? Surely that would make *me* want to sculpt something kinky."

"Like an arm is even kinky?" Kimmie says. "Leave it to Camelia to sculpt something G-rated. Now if it were me—"

"You'd be sculpting my ass?" Wes asks.

"Only if I needed a good laugh," Kimmie says.

"Funky smoking might also help explain the mysterious voices of which you speak," Wes suggests.

"Was your bedroom window locked?" Kimmie asks.

I nod, remembering how I'd had to unlock it to open the pane.

"So, it *must* have been your imagination," she continues. "Otherwise, the window would have been open, right? I mean, how do you sneak out a window and then lock it back up from the outside?"

"I know." I sigh. "It doesn't make sense."

"Wait, didn't your dad get an alarm system?" Wes asks.

"He was going to, but instead he just got the window stickers and yard signs to make it look like our house is armed."

"A crafty one, isn't he?" Wes smirks.

"Super crafty." I roll my eyes. "He also added a hyperactive motion detector in the driveway, a security camera that points toward the stairs but doesn't work, and he trimmed the bushes—"

"The biggest deterrent," Kimmie mocks.

"Of course none of it really matters," I continue, "because he constantly leaves the window in the basement open a crack, complaining that the pottery fumes give him a headache."

"Well, security measures aside, we believe you about hearing voices," Wes says, flashing me the okay sign with his fingers (as in *not* okay). "Not to mention your nagging need to sculpt Ben's body parts."

"Right," Kimmie says. "And we also believe in the Tooth Fairy, Santa Claus, and the fact that Wes is a certified stud muffin."

Wes turns to Kimmie, using his middle finger to wipe the cappuccino froth from his lip.

"You don't think it's weird that one minute I'm lying in bed, obsessing over what his scar looks like, and then, not an hour later, I sculpt his entire arm without barely even thinking about it—exactly as it should be?"

"Exactly as you *think* it should be," Wes says, correcting me.

I shake my head, confident that what I sculpted was right.

"What *I* think is weird," Kimmie begins, "is that you're trying to get us to believe that your mind and body weren't in sync—as if your hands had been invaded by the body snatchers or something."

Wes stifles a laugh with a bite of brownie.

"Bottom line," she continues, "the subconscious mind works in mysterious ways—accept it and move on."

"But it wasn't subconscious," I insist. "I wasn't sleeping."

"Maybe you were sleep*walking*," Wes suggests.

"You don't understand," I say, frustrated that they don't get it, even though I don't get it either. "This isn't the first time something like this has happened."

"You've sculpted Ben's other random body parts in the middle of the night?" Wes asks, attempting to run his fingers through his petrified hair (literally petrified: a hardened shell of gel, mousse, and dark brown spikes).

"Do tell." Kimmie leans in and bats her mascara-laden eyelashes at me.

And so I fill them in on what happened last week, when I sculpted a key for no other reason than that I felt I absolutely needed to. Later, that same day, when I got home from work, I couldn't find my key ring and my parents weren't home. "I ended up locked out of the house for more than two hours."

Wes and Kimmie stare at me—Kimmie with her ruby-stained lips hanging open in sheer bewilderment, and Wes readjusting his wire-rimmed glasses like that will make a difference, bring clarity to where there's obviously none.

"So, what are you saying?" Kimmie ventures. "You're having some sort of weird artistic premonitions?"

"Maybe," I say, biting my bottom lip, realizing how stupid the theory sounds outside the confines of my head.

"Okay, so let's just say for the sake of insanity," Wes begins, "that there was no Ben inside your house, that some weird premonition thing inside your head created that voice to lead you up the stairs, into your bedroom, so you would look out your window in the middle of the night. What do you think Ben was doing outside?"

"I don't know." I sip my cappuccino. "Maybe he wanted to talk to me."

"Then why not say hello when you called him on the phone?" Kimmie asks. "Are you sure it was even Ben outside?"

11

I shrug, not wanting to admit that, despite the streetlamp, I couldn't exactly see much detail. From what I could tell, the figure was tall, slim, and wearing a dark coat.

"Right, it could have been some other random stalker," Wes suggests.

"Like Matt, for instance," Kimmie offers. "I mean, let's face it, the boy is as free as a jailbird."

"No pun intended," Wes says, referring to Matt's punishment. At his trial two months ago, he was sentenced to just two years of probation. "Did you even *see* Ben's motorcycle?" he asks.

I shake my head and sink back in my seat, fairly confident I would have noticed his motorcycle—or at least heard it—if he were actually there.

"Hmmm . . ." Kimmie says, raising her stud-pierced eyebrow at me, perhaps not wanting to break the news— that I sound like a complete and utter nut.

The thing is, nutty theories aside, ever since Ben Carter pushed his way (literally) into my life seven months ago, things haven't quite been the same.

The first time we met, I was crossing the parking lot behind the school when a car came screeching in my direction. The next thing I knew, someone, Ben, pushed me out of the way just in the nick of time.

And in doing so, he touched me.

He rested his palm on my stomach and then something really weird happened. He stared at me with new intensity, his eyes wide and urgent, his lips slightly parted, as if he could feel something I couldn't.

It turned out that Ben had psychometry—the ability to sense things through touch. When he accidentally brushed his hand against my stomach that day, he sensed I was in danger—and beyond just the danger of getting hit by a car. The better he got to know me, the more the feeling intensified.

And he was right. I was in danger. My ex-boyfriend Matt had been plotting to keep me captive in the back of his parents' camper—in a sick and twisted scheme to win me back. Luckily, Ben had been around to save me for a second time. You'd think that would have brought us closer together.

But instead it only tore us apart.

"You want my theory?" Kimmie asks, taking a bite of éclair. "I think you're missing Ben to the kagillionth power, and so your mind is playing tricks on you."

"Let's face it, Miss Chameleon," Wes agrees, "you've got more longing in your eyes than I have stylish footwear in my closet."

"You call those things stylish?" Kimmie evil-eyes his man-clogs.

"Are you kidding? The saleslady told me I looked hot in these. I had to pay through the nose."

"Are you sure you didn't *pull* them out of your nose, too?"

"This from a girl who dresses like the Bride of Frankenstein meets June Cleaver." He gives her outfit the once-over. Today Kimmie's got on a pink and white bib-dress reminiscent of hospital volunteer wear, circa 1973.

She's also wearing a necklace made of rusted nails, with torn up fishnet stockings, combat boots, and a newsboy cap to cover her dyed-black locks.

"Jealous that I'm going to be a rich and famous fashion designer one day?" Kimmie asks him.

"A fashion designer for *Night of the Living Dead* culties maybe." Wes extends his arms and shuffles his feet to make like the sleepwalking dead.

Meanwhile, I glance out the window at the street, thinking about tomorrow. Word is Ben's finally coming back to school after having spent the past four months on his own, following Matt's arrest.

"I wonder how Ben will get treated," I venture.

Two years before our incident in the parking lot, while on a hiking trip, Ben had touched his girlfriend, Julie, and sensed that she was cheating on him. Unable to control his power, he grabbed her—hard—wanting to know more. Julie pulled away, completely spooked by the urgency of his grip. And though he tried his best to stop her, she ended up tumbling backward off a cliff, and dying almost instantly.

Ben was devastated after it happened—so much so that he spent his days avoiding touch altogether, afraid of his own powers and what he could sense. For two full years, he barely touched anyone. But then he ended up at our high school, anxious for a somewhat normal life again.

And that's when he accidentally touched me.

"I'm just surprised he's coming back at all," Wes says. "I mean, the poor boy was practically ridiculed to death."

It's true. Because of what happened with Julie, everybody at the school—the administration included—couldn't have made him feel more unwelcome. And so there were countless complaints from parents, havoc wreaked in the form of student pranks, and posers pretending to be victims of Ben's villainous ways. Nobody was willing to give him a fair chance.

Including me.

"I have my own theory as to why he wants to come back." Kimmie winks at me. "I mean, who voluntarily goes to school for the education?"

I bite my lip, hesitant to get my hopes up. The last time I saw him, when he kissed me and told me good-bye, he said that we couldn't be together, that someone like him could never be fully trusted, and that maybe someday I'd understand.

"I just hope things will go back to somewhat normal between us," I say.

"I hate to break this to you, Cam," Kimmie says, "but last I checked, feeling someone up in an effort to sense clues that could possibly cease the plot of a psycho stalker is hardly the norm."

"It's all in how you look at it, though." Wes smirks.

"You could always pretend to be in danger again," Kimmie suggests. "I could help you draft up a couple good stalker notes."

"Except he'd be able to sense it was a hoax," I say, bursting her balloon with a pin of reality.

"Not if I seriously plot to kill you," Wes says, making

his voice all sinister. He stabs his brownie with a plastic knife. "I mean, what's the worst that can happen?"

"Probation, that's what," Kimmie says, referring once again to Matt's lame-o punishment.

"The boy got away with barely a bitch-slap," Wes squawks. "I mean, honestly, you get more for public nudity these days."

"Not that you would know," Kimmie says.

"Bottom line," I segue, "at least Matt won't be coming back to school."

"But Ben *will*," she sings. "And who knows, maybe he'll touch you and sense something *really* hot."

"Even hotter than a mad stalker armed with plastic knives?" Wes jokes, continuing to stab at his brownie.

But all joking aside, I'm just hoping that Ben will talk to me—that he'll tell me it was him outside my bedroom window last night. And that he misses me just as much as I miss him.

4

*L*ATER, AT HOME, I sit up in bed and look in the mirror, once again unable to sleep. My normally bright green eyes are dull and bloodshot, and my wavy blond hair is piled high in a bed-head heap.

I just can't stop thinking about what happened the other night.

I glance out my window at the trees across the street, where I could have sworn I saw Ben. The branches are completely bare, highlighted by the streetlamp. Is it possible that I was only seeing things, that my mind concocted the whole scenario? And yet, when I close my eyes, I can still hear Ben's voice calling out to me in the basement, and then leading me up to my bedroom.

"Camelia?" a voice whispers from behind me.

I startle slightly before realizing it's my mother. She raps lightly on my open door. "It's after midnight, what are you doing up?"

I turn to face her, noticing she's still dressed in her yoga gear from work. "I could ask you the same."

She comes and sits beside me on the bed, failing to mention why she's awake, especially since she's usually asleep by ten. "Is everything okay?" she asks.

I shrug. "Another restless night, I guess."

"You had a rough sleep Friday night too, didn't you? I thought I heard you get up."

"You did?" I ask. "Did you hear anything else?"

"Like what?" Her eyes narrow.

"Nothing," I say, forcing a slight smile.

"I just think it's so wonderful that you have your sculpture," she continues. "It's important to have an outlet—a way you can express yourself and work through any stress or anxiety. That's what you did, isn't it? I thought I heard you retreat down to your studio."

"Only for a little while," I say, as though a short length of time makes a difference—makes the fact that I was up in the middle of the night less alarming.

"So, how come you're having trouble sleeping?" She gazes into the mirror at my reflection. Her henna red corkscrew curls are pushed back with a bright blue headband, emphasizing her heart-shaped face.

I shrug, tempted to tell her about Ben, but I'm not sure how happy she'd be about the possibility of him entering my world again. I mean, yes, it certainly helps that he saved my life—twice now—but still, I'm sure there's something unsettling to a parent when she hears her daughter is obsessing about a boy who was once tried for murder, regardless of the outcome of that trial.

"I think I'll try to go back to sleep," I lie.

"Want some chamomile pellets and almond milk first?"

"No thanks." I grimace, remembering how the last time she offered me one of her herbal remedies I ended up with a nasty case of hives—and on my ass, no less.

Mom kisses my forehead and tucks me in, then summons the nighttime fairies to come in through my window and hum a little tune that will lull me to sleep—just like old times.

I try not to giggle out loud. Instead I close my eyes, but I don't picture nighttime fairies.

I picture Ben.

I turn over in bed and imagine him pulling into our driveway on his motorcycle, knocking on my bedroom window, and leading me outside. In my mind, we ride along the coast, the sea-soaked air tangling the ends of my hair and making my lips taste like salt.

You'd think this image might relax me, but instead it keeps me up, reminding me of that night, last September, when I couldn't sleep—when I'd called him just before midnight to come and pick me up. I told him to take us to Knead, the pottery studio where I work, and we ended up kissing for two hours straight, right there on the worktable, the moist and gritty clay lingering on our fingertips and pasted to our skin.

It still gives me tingles.

* * *

As a result of failing to sleep more than two full hours the entire evening, I'm an absolute wreck at school.

It's the first block and I'm sitting in pottery class, trying my best to focus on my work—on everything Ms. Mazur's telling us about the instinct and emotion of a piece—but Kimmie is less than interested, instead lecturing me on my *ensemble du jour.*

"I mean, honestly Camelia, a ribbed black turtleneck with a pencil skirt? You're sixteen, not sixty. I'd have thought you'd choose something with a bit more oomph after four full months of absent longing."

"Sorry to disappoint you."

"Don't be sorry for *me.* It's *you* that I'm worried about. That ensemble is more likely to score you a discount at the supermarket on senior citizen's day than a squeeze from a certain touch boy."

"Whatever," I sigh, refusing to let her get to me.

"Of course it's not your fault," she continues in a hushed tone. "I should have called you this morning to check in about your wardrobe, but my dad had me completely distracted with the shaving of his chest. No joke: he monopolized the bathroom all morning and then had the audacity to leave the floor a hair-infested mess."

Kimmie continues to prattle on—something about having to change her tights due to stepping on said hair-infested mess, which then prompted her to change her entire outfit. I nod, trying to keep up, even though I'm much more interested in what Ms. Mazur's saying. She's allowing us to sculpt anything we want, so long as it evokes emotion in some conscious and meaningful way.

"What are you making?" Kimmie asks, rolling her clay into a giant ball.

I shrug, not really sure. I close my eyes and smooth my fingers over the mass of clay, creating slopes and grooves, trying my best to channel the emotion Ms. Mazur's talking about. After several minutes, I open my eyes, noticing how it sort of looks like I'm creating the contours of a face.

I go with it, forming the lids, pupils, and irises. Then I sculpt a box around the eyes, as though someone's looking through a window.

"Nice work, Camelia," Ms. Mazur says, standing over my shoulder. "Very intense."

I smile, flattered by the compliment, especially since intensity is precisely what I'm feeling.

"But is it as intense as the broken stiletto heel of someone who just came down the stairs at the Met?" Kimmie asks, referring to her shoe sculpture.

"Cute," Ms. Mazur says.

"Except I wasn't exactly going for cute," Kimmie squawks. "I think 'tragic' would be the word that best describes my piece."

Ms. Mazur raises an eyebrow and moves on to check out the rest of the class's sculptures. Meanwhile, I continue to work on my boxed-in eyes. About twenty minutes and a pair of eyebrows later, there's a crowd gathered around me as Ms. Mazur uses my piece to describe the look of desperation and desire.

"It's like the box represents seeing things from the

outside in—like being shut out—when all you really want is to be up close." Lily (peace-loving) Randall rests a sympathetic hand on my shoulder. Her flower-power ring grazes my neck. "Do you ever feel trapped and helpless?"

"Um, think about who you're asking," says Davis Miller, my boy-band neighbor from down the street. "It wasn't too long ago that the girl was tied up, drugged, and kept captive in the back of an old trailer."

"Right," Lily sings. "Cooooool." She continues to nod and smile at me, like being trapped is actually a good thing.

A nervous smirk inches across my lips. I try not to let it morph into a laugh—despite the topic of conversation—but then Kimmie drops her clay shoe to the floor. It lands in a messy thud against the tile.

"Holy crap!" she gasps.

But she isn't talking about her shoe.

She grabs my arm and whirls me around to face the door. It takes me a moment, but then I notice a pair of eyes staring right at me through the door's glass. You can't see his face, only his eyes.

Just like my sculpture.

"That is *so* wacky," Lily says, still nodding.

"It's like that weird key sculpture thing you were talking about," Kimmie reminds me.

I nod, trembling at the mere coincidence. I recognize the eyes right away. Dark gray, wide, and intense.

There's no doubt in my mind—they're Ben's.

I TELL Ms. MAZUR that I need to be excused to use the bathroom. But by the time I get out into the hallway, Ben is no longer there.

Instead I see John Kenneally, Kimmie's former crush, coming out of the physics lab.

"Hey," he says, nodding in my direction.

I reluctantly make my way over to say hello, the giant hallway pass—a life-size replica of a toilet plunger that a former student carved in wood shop—clutched against my work apron.

"So, how was your vacation?" he asks.

"Okay," I say, still looking around for Ben.

"Just okay?" He proceeds to fill me in on his vacation: how he had basketball practice every other day, a party to go to every single night, and back-to-back dates to fill up his weekends. "So many hearts, so little time, I tell you. The work of a heartbreaker is never done."

I resist the urge to stick my finger down my throat, and turn to gaze over my shoulder, wondering if maybe Ben has a free period this block—maybe he was coming from the library.

"Is everything okay?" John runs a hand through his dark blond hair, which is much longer and shaggier than last I noticed, like maybe he's going through some wannabe rocker phase even though he's a jock.

"Did you happen to see Ben come this way?" I ask.

"Ben? As in *Killer* Ben?" His brown eyes widen.

I give a reluctant nod, since I honestly don't feel like getting all defensive right now.

"He doesn't go here anymore," John says, like I've been living under a rock for the past several months.

"No," I correct him. "He's coming back this term. At least, that's what I heard."

"For real?" He smiles. "That guy's got some big ones, huh? If I were him, I wouldn't show my face within a thousand-mile radius of this place."

"So you didn't see him?" I snap.

"Come on, Camelia, didn't you have enough fun with your stalker-ex last term? You really need to go hanging out with full-blown killers?"

"Forget it," I say, gripping my bathroom-pass-plunger and moving down the hallway.

In the bathroom, I stand at the sink and splash some cold water onto my face. It's not John Kenneally that's got me so unhinged—at least it's not only him. I know he just speaks for the masses—that there are dozens who'll say something similar the moment they see me talking to Ben. What I don't know is why Ben's being all mysterious, first allegedly outside my house, now for certain outside my classroom.

I take a deep breath and try to get a grip. A second later, there's a knock on the bathroom door. I ignore it at first. But then there's another knock, even louder this time.

I glance in the direction of the sound, but from where I'm standing, I can't see anything. There's a wall that separates the sink area from the door.

I turn back around, but the knocking continues. It sounds like someone's beating on the door with their fist.

I grab the bathroom pass and take a couple steps toward the door, but then I hear something else. The door creaks open. I hear the hinges whine, but I still can't see.

And then the lights go off and everything goes black.

Frozen in place, I wait to hear something else, wondering if someone's come inside. I open my mouth to call out hello, but no sound comes out.

I step forward, the hall pass positioned like a baseball bat, ready to swing. "Who's here?" I shout.

No one answers.

"I know you're here." I swipe at the air, moving toward the door, but nothing interrupts my path. And so I reach out in search of the light switch on the wall. My fingers rake over the cold, hard bricks, unable to find the switch. Instead I find the doorknob and go to tear the door open, but it doesn't budge.

Like someone's locked me inside.

I pull and twist the knob with all my might, but it's no use. I let out a scream and start pounding at the door. No one comes. And there's a broken-glass feeling in my chest when I breathe.

I take a step back, trying to keep focused. The faucet drips behind me, a monotonous ping that echoes through my brain.

After a few moments, I try searching for the light switch again. This time I find it and flick it on, relieved to see that I'm alone. But then I notice a folded piece of paper at my feet. Someone must have slipped it under the door.

I reach down to grab it, my head feeling suddenly woozy. Using the wall as support, I unfold the note. The words IT ISN'T OVER YET! stab right through my heart and shake me to the core.

T HE KNOB FINALLY TURNS and I'm able to open the door. I hurry down the hallway, the note crumpled in my hands. A second later, the bell rings. The hallway fills. And my pulse continues to race. I push through the crowd and head straight to the guidance office.

Ms. Beady's door is partially closed, but I go in anyway. "I need to talk to you," I say, even though she's on the phone.

"Hold on a minute," she says into the receiver. "Camelia, can't this wait until after lunch?"

I shake my head and she pauses a moment to study me, noticing maybe how I look like I'm about to blow. Finally she tells the person she's talking to that she'll have to call them back.

"You can't just come charging in here without knocking first," she says once she hangs up. "That was an important call."

"Yeah, well, this is important too."

She gestures for me to sit in one of the two vinyl chairs facing her desk. "What's going on?" she asks.

"I should be asking you the same thing," I say, standing firmly in place.

Her eyebrows furrow like she doesn't have a clue.

"He's back," I snap. "You told me he was expelled. You told me I'd be safe here."

"Wait," she says, tucking a strand of her mousy brown bob behind her ear. "Slow down. I assume you're talking about Matt."

"Was there some other student recently on trial for kidnapping and assault with a dangerous weapon?"

"Matt isn't here," she says. "He *was* expelled. You should feel secure in knowing that he won't be back."

"He *is* back." I toss the note onto her desk.

Ms. Beady unfolds it and reads the message. "Where did you get this?"

"In the bathroom, just now. Someone shut off the lights, locked me inside, and slipped the note under the door."

"So it might not even be for you."

"Are you kidding? Look at the lettering. Look at the red marker he used. It's the same writing as the notes from before."

"Calm down," she insists, gesturing to the chair again.

"You're not going to help me, are you?"

"Of course I'm going to help. I just don't think there's any reason to jump to conclusions."

"You think it's a coincidence?"

"I think we need to discuss it further," she says. "Unfortunately, as you know, there are a lot of kids around here who like to play practical jokes, especially on the underdog—someone who might have experienced a difficulty or hardship not too long ago."

"Someone, meaning me," I say to be clear.

"It's only the first day back after the break," she says, "and already the office has given out four detentions and two in-house suspensions for practical jokes related to last semester. And it's still morning."

"But why now? Why all these pranks four months later?"

"Why do you think?" she asks, meeting my eyes.

I press my lips together, knowing it's because of Ben's return.

"Look," she continues, "I want you to know that the school takes these pranks very seriously. We want students to feel safe when they come to school, which is why, over the holiday break, we had surveillance cameras set up at the front, side, and rear entrances of the building. Principal Snell is also going to address the entire student body and issue a no-tolerance policy for pranks or practical jokes of any kind."

"What took him so long? Debbie Marcus was in a coma for over two months because of some 'pranks.' Why didn't he institute a policy then?"

"Debbie's coma wasn't exactly caused by 'pranks,' as I'm sure you know. Plus, the students in that situation were suspended for two weeks."

Two weeks as opposed to two months. "It hardly seems fair."

"We're trying our best." She lets out a sigh. "And, between you and me, a lot of kids—and parents—are really upset about Ben's return this semester, even though he has every right to be here."

"Even though he saved my life," I remind her.

She clears her throat, but refuses to respond.

"So Ben really is back?" I ask.

She nods and continues to study my face, trying to see maybe if his return upsets me too. "And since he's back, we have to prepare ourselves for a flurry of more pranks, as awful as that sounds." She gestures toward a plastic bag on her desk. Inside I can see a Hiker Barbie, backpack and all, covered in what looks like raspberry jam.

"So you think this note is a joke too?"

"That's not what I said." Her tiny gray eyes are high-lighted by way too much purple eye shadow "We can't assume anything right now. But I have a meeting with the principal set for this afternoon. I'll be sure to tell him about your experience this morning."

"Great," I say, less than grateful.

"Listen"—her face softens—"I know you're upset. You have every right to be. You've been through a lot."

"What does that have to do with me being trapped in a dark bathroom?"

"Nothing, but maybe we should schedule some further discussion." She reaches for her desk calendar.

"Forget it," I say.

"Camelia." Her lips pucker up in concern. "Try not to worry. We'll get to the bottom of this."

But I'm having serious doubts. I snatch the note right out of her hands, accidentally tearing a corner of the paper, and leave her office, even forgetting to ask for a "get out of jail free" card in the form of a late-pass.

Luckily, Mr. Swenson, a.k.a. the Sweat-man, doesn't give me a hard time. After all, I'm not the only one to come in late to chemistry.

Not thirty seconds after I take my seat, Ben arrives.

He sees me and our eyes lock. And my heart starts stomping around inside my chest. He looks just as amazing as I remember him—tall, rumpled brown hair, and eyes as dark as midnight.

"Well, hello, Mr. Carter," the Sweat-man says. "You can take your old seat." He gestures to the chair beside mine.

Ben looks at it and then up at me, but he doesn't move an inch.

"Is there a problem?" the Sweat-man asks.

My whole face blazes and I feel my palms get clammy.

Ben shakes his head and glances around the room, noticing maybe that there are no other seats available.

"Today would be nice," the Sweat-man sings.

Finally, Ben takes the seat beside mine, pausing only to nod a brief hello.

"Am I to assume you'll be continuing your pattern of lateness this term?" the Sweat-man asks him.

Ben nods and opens up his notebook.

"What a joy for the rest of us," the Sweat-man mocks.

A sprinkling of giggles erupts in the classroom, but Ben pretends not to care, instead jotting down the date. I can see the tip of his pen shake beneath his grip.

Whether the Sweat-man likes it or not, Ben has permission from the principal to arrive to all his classes late. Most people, including Principal Snell, think he suffers from claustrophobia or agoraphobia, or possibly a blending of both.

They don't know the truth about him—about his touch powers, that he comes to class late because he wants to avoid careening into people in the hallway.

Like what happened that first time he touched me.

I continue to stare at Ben's hands as he nervously folds and unfolds the edge of his notebook page. While the Sweat-man turns his back to scribble a formula for ionic bonding on the board, I scribble my own formula in the form of "Hi. Welcome back. I think we should talk."

I slide the note across the table toward him. He reads it but remains unresponsive, leaving the note right there on the table in open view. I sink back in my seat, knowing it's because he doesn't want to touch it. And the mere thought of that—of him not wanting to ever touch me again, never mind a measly scrap of paper that might carry my vibe—is like a giant sock to my gut.

I snatch the note back and stuff it into my pocket, fighting the urge to dissolve into a puddle of hot, boiling tears. Either that or chuck the note in his face.

When the bell rings, Ben finally turns to me. His

mouth is a straight, tense line. "We do need to talk," he says.

I nod, eager to ask him about the incident in the bathroom.

"Do you have time now?" he asks. "I'm free this block."

"I thought you had a free *last* block," I say, picturing him—his eyes—peering through the door glass of the art studio.

"No," he says, glancing at my mouth.

I bite my lip, completely aware that I have English next block, that I've yet to skip even one solitary class during my entire academic career, and that according to Principal Snell, skipping class is equal to defacing school property, resulting in at least one week of mandatory suspension.

But I decide to go with Ben anyway.

*I*NSTEAD OF HEADING to the cafeteria or the library, Ben leads us down the hallway behind the old computer lab. The corridors have pretty much cleared out, but I spot Debbie Marcus hustling toward the art room door at the very end, probably worried about making it in before the bell rings. She sees me, and then she notices that I'm with Ben, and a scowl forms across her face.

Last semester, Debbie was stalked as well. Everybody blamed Ben, but it turned out that her friends were the ones responsible. Like many of the clowns at this school, her friends thought it would be funny to take advantage of Ben's mysterious past. They spread a rumor that he was following her, hiding in the bushes in front of her house, and staring at her in class. They fabricated threatening notes, promising Debbie she'd be his next victim.

Eventually Debbie's mind started playing tricks on her. On a walk home from a friend's house one night, she imagined Ben was following her. She kept looking over her shoulder, stumbling out into the street, not really paying attention to where she was walking.

A car ended up hitting her as a result, and Debbie went into a coma that lasted ten full weeks. This is the first time I've seen her since the accident.

She looks different somehow—harder, thinner, a little less vulnerable maybe. Her auburn curls are held back in a barrette, and her eyes look tired; dark circles ring their steel-blue color.

After her accident, everybody assumed Ben was responsible, that he'd hit her with his motorcycle. But a witness came forward saying it was, in fact, a car that struck her, *not* a motorcycle. Unfortunately they never caught the driver.

I wave, but Debbie isn't looking at me. She's glaring at Ben. Finally the bell rings and she slips inside the classroom.

"What was all that about?" I ask Ben as he leads us away.

"I don't know," he says, shrugging it off. He steps into a storage room and opens the door wide. "I thought this might be a good place to talk. It's private, so there's less chance of you getting caught for skipping."

I hesitate a moment, noticing how dark the room is, but then I spot Principal Snell down the hallway, and quickly duck inside.

Ben closes the door behind us and tugs a chain, turning on an overhead light. The room is small, packed with shelves full of old computer printers, various cables, and reams of paper.

"Is this okay?" he asks.

I give a reluctant nod. "How do you even know about this place?"

"When people hate you as much as they hate me, you find any hole to hide in that you can."

"They don't *all* hate you."

"Oh *no?*"

I shake my head and meet his gaze. "I missed you," I say, surprising myself.

Ben's lips part, then quiver slightly, as if maybe he wants to tell me the same. Or maybe my honesty makes him nervous.

"So," I say when it's just awkward silence between us. I bite the inside of my cheek, almost wishing I could take the words back.

"Relax," he says, noticing maybe how my face is burning hot.

"I guess this is a lot harder for me than I thought. I mean, just being here . . . with you . . . trying to talk about important stuff when I really can't—"

"Concentrate?" he finishes for me. His eyes are wide and searching.

"Yeah," I say, wanting more than anything to press my face against his chest, to feel his heart pulse beneath my skin.

Ben must sense it, because he takes a couple steps back, against the opposite wall now—as far away from me as he can get.

"What's wrong?"

He looks away, as if facing me is way too hard for him. "We can't do this."

"We're not doing anything. We're just talking."

"You don't honestly believe that."

I start to tell him I do, but then stop just short of the lie.

"So, you wanted to talk?" he asks, getting right down to business.

I fish around my brain for something remotely intelligent to say. "Were you in Boston?" I ask, remembering how just before he'd left he'd mentioned possibly visiting a cousin there.

"That isn't really important. What matters now is that I'm here."

"And why *are* you here?" I say, disappointed by how closed off he's being.

"I don't know." He looks away. "Maybe I'm sick of homeschooling."

"And that's it?" An impromptu hiccup escapes from my throat. I try to cover it up with a lame little cough.

"You want a better answer?"

"I just thought there might be more to it."

"More, like what?"

"Like maybe you thought I was in danger again."

"How would I know that?" he asks. "I haven't touched you in months."

"Maybe you heard something or sensed it somehow. . . ." I pull the bathroom note from my pocket and try to hand it to him, but Ben refuses to touch it. He starts to take another step back, but between the wall and me, he's totally pinned. "Here," I say, opening the note up for him. I hold it out just inches from his face.

"'It's not over yet,'" he reads.

"I got it today, right after I spotted you spying on me in the art studio."

"Spying on you?"

"Is there something you want to tell me?"

"Where did you get that?" he asks, gesturing to the note.

"That isn't an answer." I take a step closer, and he folds his arms across his chest. "Why were you outside my house the other night?" I ask.

"What are you talking about?"

"I saw you across the street, looking up at my bedroom window."

He shakes his head and looks away again. "Not me."

"And why should I believe you?" I ask, thinking back to last September, when he lied to me about his identity—when he didn't want me to know that it was him in the parking lot that day, when he pushed me out of the way of that oncoming car.

"Believe what you want," he says, "but it wasn't me in front of your house."

"But it was you outside the art studio today," I say, to be sure. "I saw you watching me in the door glass."

"And so what does that prove? I was looking for you."

"Yes, but *why?*"

Still shaking his head, he chews his bottom lip. His forehead is sweating and his jaw is visibly clenched.

"Just say it," I demand. "I want to hear the truth."

"Okay, fine," he says, letting out a breath. "Even though I'm back, I still think we should keep our distance from one another. I think it'll make things easier."

"Easier for who?"

"For both of us."

"You can't honestly mean that," I say, suddenly feeling like the walls are closing in, like the ceiling is bearing down onto the crown of my head.

"It's for the both of us," he repeats.

I shake my head, refusing to believe it—to believe *him*—especially since he can't look me in the eye.

"But I still care about you," he continues, glancing back at the note. "I mean, we don't have to stop talking completely. We can still be lab partners."

"How generous of you."

"Don't be like that."

"Like what?" I snap. "Aren't you even a little bit concerned?"

"Did you ever think that maybe the note is a joke?"

"But look at the writing—it's the same as in Matt's notes. Nobody else saw those notes but us."

"That's what you think, but who knows? Maybe Matt showed them to someone else."

"Why would he do that? He'd risk someone telling on him."

"I just don't think you should make assumptions."

"You sound like Ms. Beady."

"Well, maybe she's right."

"Then who was outside my house?"

"I don't know." He shrugs. "Maybe a neighbor, maybe a salesperson—"

"At three in the morning?"

"I don't know," he insists.

"Something isn't right," I say, thinking about what happened in my pottery studio that night. I glance toward his arm. The treelike scar is in full view—with three branches, not four.

Just the way I sculpted it.

"If it's Matt you're worried about," he continues, "he's been ordered to keep his distance. I doubt he'd be stupid enough to come after you again."

"How do you know?"

"I don't."

"Well, I guess there's only one way to find out." I take another step toward him—so close that our faces are only inches apart. "Touch me," I say.

Ben's mouth tenses. He tries to move away, to act like it doesn't bother him, but I've got him completely cornered.

"Please." I reach out to take his hand, stopping just shy of his fingers.

"Don't," he whispers. His voice is soft and broken. "Please . . . this isn't easy for me."

"I thought you said it would make things *easier*."

Ben lets out another breath, as if trying to stay in control.

"Touch me," I repeat, staring at his lips and at the sharpness of his jaw. "And tell me if I'm in danger."

Ben finally looks at me. His eyes draw a zigzag line down my face, stopping at my mouth. He unfolds his arms and extends his palm to my shoulder. But he doesn't touch it. His fingers tremble. His breath is warm and erratic against my neck.

"I can't," he says, wiping a droplet of sweat from his cheek.

"You won't hurt me," I tell him.

"Go," he says, staring straight into my eyes, making it clear that he truly doesn't want me here. That he no longer wants any part of me.

8

January 23, 1984

Dear Diary,

My birthday sucked. My mother took Jilly to the movies. They saw Sixteen Candles and my mother kept raving about how great it was.

It's fine that they didn't ask me to go. I didn't want to see that movie anyway.

I know my mother hates me. I know she wishes I wasn't here. And I know she thinks that if I'd never come to be, my father wouldn't have left.

At least that's what she tells me. I never had the chance to ask him if it's true. Because once he left, he never looked back. And my mother's been punishing me ever since.

Love,
Alexia

9

*A*FTER SCHOOL, I head straight to Knead, even though I'm not scheduled to work. I just really want to get away.

The thing is, as soon as I unlock the door—as soon as the smell of clay and glazes hits me—I realize that maybe I've come to the wrong place. On one hand it's almost instinctive to come here—to retreat into my safe haven of clay, slip, and carving tools. And yet, the idea of sculpting anything new absolutely terrifies me right now.

I just can't shake my last three sculptures. It seems so far from coincidental now, like maybe subconsciously I already know the future somehow, but my mind doesn't want to face it. Or maybe my sculptures force me to look at what I already must know.

And yet, how could I have known I'd forget my key?

How could I have predicted that Ben's eyes would peer at me through the door of the art studio?

And how could I have known exactly how to sculpt his scar?

My head throbs just thinking about it all and what it could mean, especially coupled with what happened last September.

I never really questioned it too much at the time, but back when I was getting weird notes and packages—when Matt was plotting to take me captive—I started a new way of sculpting.

My boss, Spencer, convinced me to stop trying to control my work, to let my pottery take on its own shape for a change. A control freak by nature, I'd been sculpting bowls and bowl-like things since the first time I'd held a ball of clay. It was easy and I was good at it. But when he suggested a new approach, I thought I'd try it.

The result had been an abandoned car. I'd sculpted it over a handful of days: the dented doors, the crushed grille and bullet holes in the side. It was the same car I'd spotted in the trailer park where Matt had kept me captive . . . right down to the missing wheels.

Should I be calling that a coincidence too?

To add to my confusion, it doesn't help that Ben swears it wasn't him in front of my house the other night. So, is he lying? Was I imagining things?

Could it possibly have been Matt?

I look toward the back of the studio, wondering if I should turn around and head out the door. It's not like anyone's actually seen me yet. The place looks empty, and Spencer's work light is switched off.

I turn to leave, only to find that I'm not alone after all. There's a boy standing just inside the door, staring right at me.

I take a step back, my heart beating fast.

"Are you okay?" he asks. He's about my age or a little older, with wavy brown hair and olive-toned skin.

"Sorry," he says, approaching me slowly. "I didn't mean to startle you."

"Where's Spencer?"

"Downstairs, loading the kiln. Are you okay?" he repeats.

"Where did you come from?" I ask, bumping into the worktable behind me. I look toward the door, knowing I would have heard him come in.

"Medland, originally." He smiles. "It's about a three-hour drive from here."

"You know what I mean."

"I was behind the counter. You walked right by me." He extends his hand for a shake, but I don't move an inch. "I'm Adam. Spencer hired me to pull molds." He flexes his muscle to be funny.

"How come Spencer didn't mention a new hire to me?"

"I don't know; why don't you ask him?" He gestures behind me. Spencer's there.

"I take it you two have met," Spencer says, wiping a smear of slip on his jeans.

"Not really," I say.

"Camelia, Adam; Adam, Camelia," Spencer says, still wiping. There's a streak of green glaze down his scruffy face.

"Well, it's a pleasure to meet you, Camelia." Adam extends his hand again. This time I shake it, noticing his sweaty palm.

"Camelia's an ace at throwing bowls," Spencer says. "Don't let her demure demeanor fool you."

"Hardly demure," Adam says. "For a second there, I thought she was gonna take my head off."

"You startled me."

"No worries," Adam says. "We're working together now; I'll let you make it up to me somehow."

"You'll *let* me?"

"Sure," he says. "I'm new to the area, so I might be needing a tour guide."

"How new?" I ask.

"This is my first semester at Hayden."

"The community college?"

He nods. "And you?"

"I'm a junior, actually . . . at the high school. That's where Spencer and I met. He was subbing for my pottery teacher."

"And I couldn't take my eyes off her soup bowls." Spencer winks. "I'm telling you, this girl's got talent."

"Can I see some of your work?" Adam asks.

"Maybe some other time. I have a soup bowl to throw," I joke.

"Well, be sure it has big round coils." Spencer winks again. "The extruder's all fixed, by the way."

"The extruder is for wusses," I say, referring to pottery's version of a pasta maker, complete with various attachments that can transform even the biggest wads of clay into long noodlelike strands.

While he and Adam head off to the back room, I use the wire cutter to slice myself a fist-size clump of clay. I'm determined to sculpt something simple and predictable today—something, ironically, exactly like a soup bowl.

I know exactly the way I want my bowl to look: a bubblelike base with a tulip-turned rim, big enough for flowers, but not for a full bowl of fruit. I end up working for well over an hour, rolling my coils out by hand, stacking them atop the oval base, and then weaving them together to form ripples along the sides. The whole familiar process of it helps me relax—to concentrate on something simple—even though, for some reason, despite how supposedly foolproof coil pots are, I can't seem to get mine the way I want it. It looks more like a bottle than an actual pot. The tulip spout has more of a screw-cap look. And the pot's much taller and thinner than I'd imagined—more like a water bottle or a very narrow vase.

I sit back on my stool, wondering how this happened. I mean, I used to have so much control over my bowls. I knew exactly the way they'd turn out before I even began.

Instead of letting it bother me, I decide to call it a day and add the finishing touch. On the surface of the bottle, for no other reason than I think it might look good—might provide an interesting contrast to the shape of the bottle—I use a carving knife to draw a pomegranate.

I'm just about finished perfecting the starlike end of

the stem, when I feel someone's watching me. I turn around, startled to find Adam.

"Hey," he says, standing only a few feet away. "I didn't want to interrupt."

"How long have you been standing there?"

"Just a few seconds. What are you working on?"

"Nothing much," I say, about to turn back around. But that's when I notice what's in his hand.

I see the pomegranate first. It adorns the front of his juice bottle, under a label that reads "Perfectly Pomegranate."

"Are you okay?" he asks, obviously noticing the confusion on my face.

I look back at my sculpture—same bottle shape, same tubular ripples. Even the angle of the pomegranate is the same—the stem cocked to the right.

He takes a sip from the bottle. Meanwhile, I hurry to cover my sculpture with some plastic.

"Is something wrong?"

"Where did you get that?" I ask, wondering if maybe I saw the bottle before, if maybe, subconsciously, it stuck somehow.

"Where did I get *what*?"

"That bottle," I demand. "Did you have it before, when you were standing by the doorway, when I first came in?"

"Um, no," he says, his eyebrows arched, like I'm full-on crazy. "I got it out of my bag just a second ago. Are you sure you're all right?"

I shake my head, feeling my face flash hot.

"Do you want a sip?" He holds the bottle out as an offering, but I can't even look at it now.

"I want to get back to my work," I mutter, feeling like an absolute freak—and knowing I must sound like one too.

Finally Adam gets the message and turns away, leaving me alone.

IO

*J*END UP COMING STRAIGHT HOME after Knead, determined to get to the bottom of things. I tear off my coat, drop my books to the floor, and rush to my computer. I start by Googling the word "psychometry," recognizing some of the sites I'd visited when I first learned about Ben's powers.

Most of the sites say the same thing. People who have psychometric powers experience them in different ways. Some are able to touch an object and know where it's been or what its history is. Others, like Ben, can touch a person or thing and get an image inside their head—an image that helps foretell the future.

I navigate through a bunch of sites, learning more and more about psychometry—how some people, instead of getting a mental image, taste different flavors or imagine specific textures inside their mouths, all relevant to what they touch. And then there are those who hear things—

50

like music, voices, and other sounds—whenever they touch something.

I lean back in my chair, thinking how that's sort of like what happened to me when I was in the basement, sculpting Ben's arm, when I heard his voice calling out to me, leading me up into my bedroom.

I spend another full hour reading everything I can, learning tidbits about how psychometric powers can be developed, but still unable to find the answer to what I'm really looking for: Can the power be transferred from person to person?

I know it sounds completely crazy, and there's absolutely nothing in these Web pages that even suggests such an occurrence. But how else do I explain what's been going on?

"Camelia?" my dad calls, knocking on my open bedroom door. "Dinner's ready."

I swivel around to face him. "I'm not really hungry."

"Since when does hunger have anything to do with your mom's cooking?"

"You mean her *not* cooking," I say, referring to her latest obsession with raw cuisine. The stove has become more of a storage space than a place to prepare food.

"She's making raw pizza."

"Sounds delish," I lie.

"That's what I told her. Please"—he shudders, flashing me a container of Tums—"don't make me do it alone."

"Okay." I cave. "I'll be there in a few."

But no sooner do I say it than my cell phone rings. It's

Kimmie, announcing that her parents are driving her crazy and she's coming over—*stat*.

I hang up and break the news to Dad—that I won't be joining them for dinner after all. He's a little ticked at first, but softens up when I promise him a trip to Taco Bell later, my treat.

When Kimmie arrives, we camp out in my room and talk over bags of barbecue chips and Reese's peanut butter cups—essentials she's brought along. She tells me that her parents are fighting hard core, yelling at each other at all hours of the night.

"And then the other day," she continues, "I was working on some of my designs, something from my Bad Girl & Breakfast line." She gestures to her outfit, which appears to be a silk black pillowcase with cutouts for the neck and arms. A chain-link belt is strapped around her waist. "And my dad told me I was wasting my time."

"I'm sorry," I say, reaching out to touch her arm.

She shrugs, wiping a mascara-stained tear from her cheek. "It's like he's not happy about anything anymore, especially when it comes to me and Nate. It's even worse for Nate. The kid's only eight years old. He looks up to my dad like he's a freakin' superhero or something."

"Well, I hate to get all Oprah on you," I say, giving her arm a good squeeze, "but it's not your fault. Whatever your parents are going through has nothing to do with you and your brother."

"Tell my dad that. He's constantly complaining that

money's tight because he's stuck spending it all on us. Meanwhile, my mom's so busy trying to make him happy. Trying to look ten years younger and fit into clothing two sizes too small. Now she's reading all this weird couples stuff. Books about the 'sensual years' and satisfying your man. It's all so gross."

"I'm sorry," I repeat, not really knowing what else to say.

"Whatever," she says, blotting her black tears with a tissue. "I mean, at least it gets them off my back, right?"

"Is there anything I can do?"

"You're already doing it," she says, gesturing around my room with a chip. "Just don't kick me out, okay?"

"You can stay here as long as you want."

"What were you up to, by the way?" She glances toward my computer.

"We don't have to talk about me."

"Are you kidding? I'm so done talking about my parents. Let's move on to something normal. Or at least as normal as your life can possibly be."

"Exactly," I sigh.

"Do I smell something scandalous?"

I take a deep breath and tell her about the note I got in the bathroom today, about my conversation with Ben in the storage room, and then I segue into what happened at Knead with the bottle and the new boy.

"Was he hot?"

"You're missing the point."

"Right." She nods. "The point is that I can't believe

you played ten minutes in the closet with Ben and you didn't even touch him."

"More like *he* didn't touch *me*. But you're still missing the point."

"And you don't think there's any possibility that all this sculpture stuff could be a coincidence? I mean, weirder things have happened—like with me, for example. I was once having these dreams about some random girl from grammar school, someone I hadn't seen in years. And then, a week later, I bumped into her."

"Sounds like a premonition."

"More like selective memory. A couple weeks before the dreams started, my mom had shown me a newspaper article about the girl. I'd completely forgotten about it, because, let's face it, the girl and I had nothing in common, what with her Gap attire and all—"

"Sort of like mine?"

"The *point* is that I may have forgotten seeing the article, but obviously my subconscious mind didn't, because for whatever reason I dreamed about her. The fact that I saw her later—now, *that* was a coincidence."

"Well I'm done calling what's been happening a coincidence. Plus, I heard Ben's voice in my basement," I remind her. "How do you explain that?"

"Insanity?"

"I'm being serious here. I mean, even *you* said the whole incident in sculpture class was like what happened when I sculpted my house key."

"Well, I honestly think you're asking the wrong

person," she says. "You really need to talk to Ben again. If anyone would know about all this seeing-the-future stuff it would be him."

"Maybe you're right."

"And maybe it's catching."

"Psychometric powers?"

"You never know," she says, rubbing my leg, hoping some power will rub off on her. "I'd kill to know who I'll be taking to the prom."

"I can't think that far ahead."

"Because of the note?" She pulls it from under the chip bag.

"I just don't want to do this again," I whisper, feeling a knot form in my gut. "Do you think it's a joke?"

"That's my vote. I mean, just think about all the pranks that went on last semester. Someone obviously saw you go into the bathroom and thought it'd be funny to harass you. Do you remember anyone specific in the hallway?"

"John Kenneally."

Her face freezes, midchew. "I really doubt it'd be him."

I roll my eyes, wondering why she continues to defend him. All last September, John was completely obnoxious to Ben, harassing him whenever he had the chance. Somehow, despite all that obnoxiousness, Kimmie still found John attractive, telling me on a fairly regular basis how hot she thought he was.

"And you don't think there's any chance it could be Matt?" I ask, pointing out the similar lettering on the note.

"Are you serious?"

"Do I look like I'm joking?" I can feel the flush of my face.

"There's a restraining order against Matt."

"Talk about a joke."

"Matt wouldn't be that stupid."

"Then what about the similar lettering?"

"So the person used a red marker and wrote in capital letters, big deal. If I were writing a stalker note, I'd probably write in all caps too."

"Oh would you now?" I manage a smirk.

"Actually, I'd probably type it instead. I'd also wear gloves, so that no one could trace my fingerprints. And I'd make all my stalker calls from random phone booths."

"Sounds like you've got it all planned out."

"Honey, I've got more plans than Wes has ugly shoes."

"And that's a lot." I laugh.

"It sure is," she says with a sigh.

II

February 7, 1984

Dear Diary,

Yesterday in art class, Mrs. Trigger made me rip up my painting and throw the pieces away in the garbage. It was a portrait of me with bright red streaks running from both my wrists. At least that's what I told Mrs. Trigger: bright red streaks from a bottle of spilled nail polish, instead of trickles of blood.

Mrs. Trigger said the streaks, nail polish or not, looked too scary and that girls my age should be painting pretty things like ponies and fields full of wildflowers.

But that's just not me.

I use art as a way to get things out. Though just about everything I draw or paint seems to come out anyway. I mean, it comes true, which is one of the reasons I think maybe I should stop doing art altogether. Except knowing what happens before anyone else makes me feel sort of special, when I have nothing else to feel special about.

Love,
Alexia

FTER KIMMIE LEAVES, and after my dad and I have taken a trip to Taco Bell to fill up on nonraw food goodness, I lie awake in bed wondering if I should take Kimmie's advice and give Ben a call.

It's a little after eleven and I can't sleep. I'm almost tempted to go downstairs to my studio. Instead I grab a random book off my shelf—*Teens, Tweens, & Yogi Machines*, obviously something my mother bought me. There's a lengthy forward about finding your inner *om*. I try reading the first few pages, but I can't concentrate. Finally I reach for my cell phone and dial Ben's number.

"Hi," he answers on the first ring.

"Did I wake you?"

"No. I couldn't sleep."

"Me neither."

There's silence between us for several seconds—just

the sound of each other's breath—but then a few moments later a car alarm screeches in the background, on his end of the line.

"Where are you?" I ask.

"Riding around. I just stopped at a gas station."

"Where?"

More silence.

"You don't want to tell me?" I ask.

"It's not that."

"Then what?"

Still, he doesn't answer.

"Forget it," I say, my heart beating fast. "I was just hoping that maybe we could talk. Not over the phone, though. I need to see you."

"Can't it wait until tomorrow?"

"Not really," I say. "It's sort of important."

There's another long pause on the other end. Meanwhile, I can hear police sirens blaring on his end of the phone. They seem to be getting closer to wherever Ben is.

"What's going on there?"

"Okay," he says, ignoring the question. "I'll swing by your house."

He hangs up and I reach for my coat, hoping we can go for a ride. Not two minutes later, I hear the rev of his engine from down the street. I open my window wide as he pulls up in front of my house, steps off his bike, and removes his helmet.

He looks even better than earlier today. A black leather

jacket clings to his chest, and his hair is rumpled to perfection. He gazes up at me, his silhouette highlighted by the moon.

I wave, barely able to hold myself back—to not go tearing out the window and running into his arms.

"Hey," he says, when he gets within earshot.

"Hey," I repeat.

He smiles slightly, as if he wants to talk to me too, as if caught off guard in the moment—like the way things used to be.

"So, shall we go someplace?" I ask.

"We don't have to," he says. "You can just say what you have to tell me right here . . . right now."

My pulse stirs, almost tempted to invite him in, just imagining him inside my room. I peer over my shoulder at my bedroom door, noticing how my schoolbag is caught in the doorway.

"Please," I whisper, suddenly eager to get away, to not have to worry about my parents busting in and catching us together. "Can you take us somewhere?"

He looks toward his motorcycle. "How about we go for a walk? The streets are a little slippery tonight. I wouldn't be able to forgive myself if we wiped out."

I know it's a lame excuse, that he doesn't want to go for a ride because that would mean I'd have to touch him. I crawl out my window, shutting the curtains and drawing the pane closed behind me. Then I hop to the ground, completely aware that Ben doesn't help me.

We walk down the length of my street, passing by

Davis Miller's house on the right. His bedroom light's still on. Maybe he can't sleep either.

It's quiet and awkward between Ben and me again; there's just the sound of our boots as they crunch over gravel and patches of snow. I glance at his hands as he crams them inside his pockets, remembering that night at Knead last September, when his clay-soaked fingers slid up the back of my T-shirt, against my skin, turning my insides to putty.

"I'm sorry about earlier," Ben says, breaking the silence. "I didn't mean to sound like an asshole."

"You didn't," I lie. Except maybe it's only a half-lie.

"I really care about you." He stops to face me. His lips are chapped from the cold.

"I'm glad," I say, feeling my cheeks blaze. "Because I really care about you too."

Standing beneath the streetlight, he pauses a moment to study me—my hair as the wind whips through it, the tearing of my eyes from the cold, and how I can't stop nibbling my lips. At least I think that's what he's looking at.

"So, what did you want to talk about?" he asks, walking again.

"Touching." I look over at his face to check for his reaction.

"You know I can't touch you."

"I know you don't *want* to touch me," I correct him, "but that's not what I wanted to talk to you about."

"So, what then?"

"I was just kind of wondering"—I take a deep

breath—"if the power of psychometry can be trans-ferred from person to person."

He stops again, his face scrunching up like he's gen-uinely confused. "What are you talking about?"

"Is that a no?"

"It's not a virus," he continues. "Psychics don't just sneeze and pass their power along to the person standing next to them."

My face turns hotter, fully aware of how crazy the whole theory sounds. Ben stares at me, waiting for some explanation. Meanwhile, my palms are clammy and my ears begin to sting from the chill.

"What's going on?" he insists.

"It's hard to explain," I venture, "but all this weird stuff has started happening to me."

"Like what?"

And so I tell him about the key and the bottle sculp-ture, how I sculpted his arm, and then about his eyes through the door glass.

"That's it?" He smiles as if relieved. "A bottle? A door key? They're pretty common objects, don't you think?"

"Not really," I say. "Not when one of those objects had a very specific pomegranate label."

"Maybe you saw the label in a store. Maybe for some reason you subconsciously retained it. It could be the same thing with the key. Maybe part of you knew you'd left it at home."

"But then how do you explain all that other stuff—the stuff I sculpted about you?"

He swallows hard; I watch the motion in his neck. "I don't know," he says, trying to cram his hands deeper into his pockets, even though they've reached the bottom seam. "Maybe you just sculpted that stuff because you're missing the way things used to be."

"I do miss it." I wait for him to return the sentiment, but instead he stays silent.

I look away, trying not to show my emotion, even though I can feel it in my eyes, a deep and penetrating sting.

"Are you okay?" he asks.

I nod.

He must sense how upset I am, because we end up moving forward again, taking a turn onto Columbus Street.

The street where Debbie Marcus was hit.

"Maybe we should call it a night," I say, feeling a chill snake down my spine.

"Are you sure?"

I nod and turn back, my pace quickening, eager to get home, to get away—when only minutes before I couldn't wait to be with him.

We walk for several blocks in silence—just the sound of our steps and the panting of breath as Ben hurries to keep up. It doesn't take long before we're back in front of my house. I mumble a faint good-bye and head back toward my window. Meanwhile, a storm of tears rages behind my eyes.

"Camelia, wait," Ben calls.

I reluctantly stop and turn to face him. Our motion

across the driveway has triggered the spotlight.

"Don't be like this," he says.

"Like what? Don't feel anything? Be more like you?"

Ben takes a couple steps toward me, as if he wants to give me a hug, but instead he stops. His lips move, as if to form words, but no sound comes out, like maybe he doesn't know what to say either.

Or maybe what he has to say is too painful for me to hear.

"If I can't *be* with you, then I can't be *with* you," I say finally, wiping my eyes on my sleeve. "I can't pretend like what we had didn't exist."

Ben looks away. His eyes are as red as mine now. "I'm sorry," he whispers.

"I'm sorry too." A crumbling sensation fills my chest. I turn back around, half hoping he'll stop me again.

But instead I hear his motorcycle rev, followed by the sound of him pulling away.

*A*FTER BEN LEAVES, I try to hold it all together so I can make it back inside my house. I head for my bedroom window. But then I come to a sudden halt.

The window is wide open, the curtains billowing in the wind. I could have sworn I shut it on my way out. I'm almost positive I drew the curtains closed.

I approach the window slowly and peek inside my room. From where I'm standing, everything appears to be completely normal, just as I left it. I look back over my shoulder. The street is quiet and dark.

Using all the strength in my arms, I pull myself up and onto the sill, noticing a large red envelope on the floor of my room.

I crawl inside and pick it up, wondering if maybe my parents came in here while I was out. Maybe one of them dropped it and now they know I snuck away. I look toward my door. It's still closed. My schoolbag is still wedged in the doorway.

I glance back at the open window and move quickly to shut it. It sticks, even when I bear down with all my weight. My fingers shaking, I continue to push downward, until the muscles in my arms ache. Finally the window closes and I'm able to lock it shut. The spotlight in the driveway is still illuminated, as if maybe someone's out there.

I draw the shade down, close the curtains, and sit on the edge of my bed, trying to ease the clamoring inside my chest. Part of me hopes that it was Ben who left the envelope somehow. Maybe there was stuff he wanted to tell me, stuff that he couldn't say to my face.

I tear it open, barely able to get my fingers to work right. Two photos sit inside.

The first is a snapshot of a shrine. Bouquets of flowers decorate what appears to be the top of a cliff. There's also a framed picture of a brown-haired girl, probably a few years younger than me.

My stomach lurches. I take a closer look and see a dirt trail that runs through the forest, straight to the very top—the place where Ben and Julie went hiking that day. The spot where she fell backward.

And died almost instantly.

The second snapshot was taken in the same area; the shrine is visible in the distance. There's a grouping of rocks splattered over with graffiti. I can only make out a few of the words—the ones that name Ben a killer, a coward, and telling him to rot in hell.

My hands still shaking, I turn the photos over. The graffiti one is blank, but the picture of the shrine has a message for me. The words stare up in angry red letters: LET'S GO FOR A HIKE.

14

THIS CAN'T BE HAPPENING AGAIN.

The photos pressed in my hands, I do my best to hold it together—to not cry out at the top of my lungs and wake up my parents.

I grab the edge of my dresser for stability, unable to stop the rush of questions storming through my mind, shaking up my world.

My forehead is sweating. As I reach for a tissue, I notice that the glass on my bedside table's been knocked over. There's a pool of water on the rug, trailing beneath my bed, which makes me realize—maybe I'm not alone.

A giant knot forms in my chest. I try to breathe it away, but it only gets tighter. I drop the photos on the bed and grab a letter opener from my desk, the tip positioned to fight.

Slowly I bend to the floor, imagining Matt. His face flashes across my mind: his teal-blue eyes, that wicked grin, and the way he grabbed me that day—when he twisted my arm behind my back and told me he'd been following me, and that we belonged together.

The letter opener clenched in my hand, I reach out for the bed-skirt fabric. In one quick motion, I pull it upward.

At first I see Matt, his menacing glare still alive in my mind. But then I realize I'm alone, that my eyes are playing tricks on me, and that I seriously need to calm down.

I back away and check inside the closet. It's empty, too. And so I stand in the center of my room and count to ten, trying to decide what to do. Part of me wants to go tell my parents. Another part thinks I should just call Kimmie.

Except, I really don't feel like hearing Kimmie tell me that this is yet another stupid joke. And I hate the idea of being kept under my parents' protective scrutiny. For three full months following Matt's arrest, I could barely even go to the bathroom by myself without my mom knocking on the door to ask me if I was all right, if I needed any help, and what was taking me so long. Things are just starting to get back to normal.

At least I thought they were.

I grab the photos and the envelope and make my way downstairs to my pottery studio, remembering something I read about psychometry online—how you can develop your senses through practice and meditation. I concentrate on the photos and the note for a good twenty minutes, before cutting myself a fresh mound of clay.

Keeping my fingers moist, I turn the clay over and

over against my board, until I feel ready to sculpt. I close my eyes, trying to keep my mind open like the article online suggested. After several minutes, I've pretty much convinced myself that I'm trying too hard. Random images pop into my head: seashells, paintbrushes, bed linens. . . .

Still, I keep trying, listening for any subtle noises, remembering what I read—how some people who experience psychometry are able to hear sounds or voices relevant to whatever they touch.

But I don't hear anything. And the only image that sticks—the one that presses into my mind's eye and makes my blood stir—is a swordfish jumping out of the ocean.

Not knowing what else to do, I sculpt the image, fairly convinced it's a waste of time. Still, once it's done, I sit back and study the shape, repeating the word *swordfish* over and over again inside my head, searching for any pertinence at all.

Meanwhile, I can't stop thinking about my conversation with Ben. He told me that psychometry isn't contagious. But what I didn't tell him was that when I sculpted his arm, I was able to hear his voice.

Would that have changed his mind?

I gaze back at the photos, not knowing what to believe, feeling a sickly sensation in the pit of my stomach. I remind myself that Matt was expelled, that the court ordered a restraining order against him. Still, my mind whirs, wondering if only the photos were from him, and the bathroom note was from someone else. But that doesn't make sense either, especially considering that the bathroom note warned me that it's not over yet, and then later the same day I get these snapshots.

I run my fingers over the shrine photo, focusing on the picture of Julie. She's pretty, with long dark hair held back with a ribbon, and wide green eyes that squint when she smiles. She looks happy in the photo, like falling off a cliff couldn't be farther from her thoughts . . . And yet there she is, her picture among all those weeping roses.

A second later my cell phone rings, startling me. I pull it from my pocket and place it up to my ear. "Hello?"

It's silent on the other end, like someone's just listening.

"Hello?" I repeat, louder this time.

Still no one answers. I hang up and check the caller ID. It's Kimmie's number, and so I call her right back.

"It's one a.m.," she answers. Her voice is a groggy mess.

"*You're* the one who called *me*."

"Um, no I didn't."

"Yes you did." I check my phone screen again. "My phone says you're the last one who called."

"Yeah, but that was at like eleven thirty."

"Really?" I look back at the screen; it says I have one missed call. So why didn't I hear it ring? "My phone rang just now, but nobody was on the other end."

"I freaking hate cell phones. I mean, I love them, but I also hate them, you know? With mine, you can barely hear the person talking on the other end. It's totally inaudible. And don't even get me started with my caller

ID. Half the time it doesn't even work."

"Were you sitting on your phone maybe?" I ask, remembering a time when I accidentally dialed Wes's number that way.

"Excuse me?"

"Forget it."

"Gladly." She laughs. "So what's up?"

"Shouldn't I be asking you the same?"

"Oh, right." More laughing. "I called you first. Are you seriously still up, by the way?"

"You don't exactly sound like you're sleeping either." At least her voice no longer sounds groggy.

"Guilty as charged. I've been up working on some design stuff. I couldn't sleep so I thought I'd hem, but then my hem came out crooked. I really need to give your mom's chamomile pellets a try."

"It happened again," I say, all but cutting her off at the hem.

"You got hives on your ass?"

"No, I got another note."

"Seriously?"

I spend the next ten minutes filling her in about the photos, the open window, and how Ben and I went for a walk.

"And now he wants to take you for a hike?" she asks.

"I didn't say the photos came from him."

"But it's totally possible. I mean, he was right there. He had the perfect opportunity to slip something by you when you weren't looking."

"Why would he do that? I mean, the photos make him look like a killer."

"Maybe he wants you to see him that way."

"Be serious."

"I'm trying," she sighs. "You can't honestly expect me to get into the twisted mind of a stalker at one in the morning."

"But you don't really think of him that way, right?" I glance at the shrine photo again, admiring Julie's face, her sweet smile and bubbly cheeks. Her hand rests under her chin, making her look totally approachable, like someone I might have been friends with.

"You know what's really weird?" she says, ignoring the question. "The fact that you got photos again. It's like someone's copying Matt."

"I know," I say, thinking back to last September, when I was receiving candid photos of myself on a regular basis—snapshots of me on the street, in front of the school, shopping in town. . . .

All to prove that I was being watched.

"Of course, if it's just a copycat, then it probably *is* a joke," Kimmie says.

"Except it's not exactly a copycat. I mean, the photos aren't of me this time."

"Which brings me back to Ben," she says. "Maybe he *was* the one who left them. Maybe he thought it would put a little distance between you. He did say he wanted space."

"But that would sure be an extreme way to get it, don't

you think? I mean, he might not want to be with me, but he still cares what I think about him. At least I hope he does."

"A small sacrifice for space."

"Okay, so now you *are* thinking like a killer," I say, still refusing to buy into her theory.

"It's a gift." She giggles, but then lets out a gasp. "I totally just stabbed myself with a needle."

"Time to put all sharp objects away."

"Thanks for reminding me why I called," she says. "I thought you'd want to know what I heard about Matt. He's in Louisiana. No joke. I made Todd McCaffrey repeat it three times. Todd's my new flavor-of-the-month, by the way. I mean, seriously, have you seen the way he fills out a pair of jeans? He puts the Chiquita in my banana."

"What's Matt doing in Louisiana?"

"Habitat for Humanity. He went down there—to help rebuild houses. Apparently he's trying to redeem himself, do something noble after making your life a living hell, blah, blah, blah."

"Wow," I say, somewhat surprised by this bit of news, and not really knowing how to feel about it.

"Wow, indeed. Todd even asked me out for this weekend. What do you think about Spanish food followed by salsa lessons for a first date?"

"Isn't Todd still dating Debbie Marcus? I mean, the poor girl just came out of a coma."

"They actually broke up *pre*-coma," she corrects. "Pre-hit-and-run, to be exact. Apparently Debbie was super high-strung and extra annoying. According to Todd, that is."

"Interesting."

"To say the least. Anyway, I just thought you should know about Matt since you were all wigged about that weird bathroom note. The boy is definitely out of the picture, so maybe you can finally get some rest."

I let out a breath, indeed relieved, but still not quite ready to call the whole thing a joke.

*T*HE FOLLOWING DAY AT SCHOOL, I decide to create my own degree of space. With Matt supposedly away in Louisiana, I'm feeling a bit more at ease—a bit more willing to see how things play out before I tell my parents everything.

Not even two seconds down the corridor, I spot the gag-du-jour. Someone's doused a G.I. Jane doll with what appears to be red corn syrup and hung it from a jump-rope-turned-noose, so that it dangles down in the center of the hallway.

There's a crowd of people around it, including John Kenneally, Todd McCaffrey, Davis Miller, and a bunch of lemmings from the soccer team. They bat the doll back and forth like a game of handball, like they have nothing better to do than show the entire school how ignorant they are.

It's all I can do to walk past them—to not tear the

thing down and call them out as the losers they are. Except, as twisted as it sounds, there's also a part of me relieved by the display—relieved that I'm not the only victim of the hysteria, that these stupid jokes seem to be around every corner.

Two blocks later, instead of taking my usual seat in chemistry, I ask the Sweat-man for a new lab partner.

"Rules are rules," the Sweat-man chirps. "Whomever you sat with on the first day of school is your lab partner for life—or at least until the end of the year. Pick a better partner next year for physics."

"Please," I insist, keeping my voice low. "Things haven't exactly been great between Ben and me."

"How so?" he asks, oddly eager for the juice.

"It's sort of complicated," I say, almost wishing I'd never asked.

The Sweat-man makes a tsk-tsk sound with his tongue, and then runs his fingers through his oily dark hair. I lean back to avoid the flurry of dandruff as it falls to his shoulders. "Well, then let's uncomplicate things, shall we?" He turns toward the class.

Ben has finally arrived—only three minutes late today. He takes a seat in his usual spot, right beside mine, and stares straight at me.

"Is there anyone who would like to swap lab partners with Camelia?" the Sweat-man continues.

Nearly everyone in the class turns to look at Ben, but no one says anything. Ben's mouth parts in surprise, which only makes me feel worse.

"Anyone? Anyone?" the Sweat-man asks. An amused smile has inched up his face.

Ben continues to stare at me, his eyes slightly swollen.

"Going once, going twice . . ."

Still no one speaks, and I'm suddenly relieved—as if I can just go take my seat now, as if things could ever possibly go back to normal.

I gather up my books and move in that direction. But then Rena Maruso raises her hand. "I'll switch," she says.

"Sold!" the Sweat-man shouts, using a steel beaker as a makeshift gavel.

Rena gets up and crosses the room, taking the seat beside Ben's. *My* seat. Meanwhile, I clench my teeth, reminding myself that this is for the best—and that this is what Ben wanted too. He all but said so last night.

While the Sweat-man turns away to write something on the board, I slide into my new seat at the front of the class, and then glance back at Ben.

He's looking at me too. Part of me wants to mouth an "I'm sorry." But before I can, he glances away, like the moment is completely over for him.

Like maybe our relationship is too.

A FTER SCHOOL, I head straight to Knead, relieved that I have to work, that I'll be busy setting up for classes and unloading the kiln and won't have time to dwell on the dysfunction that is my life.

Actually, after discussing the whole Ben situation with Kimmie and Wes at lunch earlier, I'm feeling a smidgen better. Both agreed that Ben had his chance, that my asking to switch lab partners was the right thing to do.

"You didn't just ask to switch partners," Wes declared, driving the point home by punching the air with his juice box. "You took a piece of your life back. You were saying 'I am desirable,' 'I have self respect,' 'I deserve more.'"

"I am a Dr. Phil wannabe," Kimmie mocked.

"You should be celebrating your liberation," Wes continued, "not dwelling on what *Ben* might be feeling. I ask you: what were *you* feeling last night when he drove away and left you out in the cold?"

"The cold, quite literally," Kimmie said. "It must have been twenty below last night."

"Like crap," I answered, forking through a plate full of pasty red mush, which the cafeteria ladies had dubbed American Chop Suey. "I felt like crap."

"Precisely," Wes said. "And now it's time to move on, to extract the crap from your life."

"Right," I said, less than enthusiastic, but still knowing that he was right.

And so now, nearly four hours later, as I lay the work boards out on the table for today's wheel-throwing class, I chant Wes's mantra inside my head, telling myself that I'm desirable, deserving, and oozing with self-respect and admiration. For some reason, it helps me relax.

But then I feel a hand on my back.

I whirl around, dumping a cup full of paintbrushes in the process.

Adam is standing right behind me. "Sorry," he says, moving to pick up the brushes. "I forgot how jumpy you are. For the record, I've been trying to get your attention for the past five minutes."

"What are you talking about?"

"I've been calling your name, but it's like you don't hear me. Like you're someplace else maybe." He sets the cup of paintbrushes back on the table. "Are you sure you're okay?"

"I'm fine," I say, trying to be nice. "Did you need something?"

"Mold bands." He flips a strand of his wavy dark hair

from in front of his eyes. "I was just wondering if you knew where Spencer keeps them."

"In the box. By the kiln downstairs."

"Great." He ventures a smile and studies my face, making sure that I'm okay. "Can I give you a hand setting up? I should probably learn this stuff at some point."

I shake my head but then reconsider, because it seems like he's really trying to redeem himself. I hand him a stack of boards and he follows my lead.

"So what do people do for fun around this town?" he asks, adding the final touch to our otherwise fully stocked table—a centerpiece in the form of sculpting tools, sponges, and spray bottles.

"You mean besides pulling twisted pranks on people?"

"Um, yeah." He smirks. "Besides that."

"Sorry," I say, shaking my head at my idiotic response.

"Rough day?"

"Rough year."

"Hence the jumpiness?"

"I suppose," I sigh.

"Something you want to talk about?"

"Something I want to *forget* about," I say.

"Well then, how about Friday night? Are you free? I promise not to pull any twisted pranks."

"I don't know," I say, completely taken aback. "I mean, I don't think so."

"You're busy?"

"Not exactly."

"You have a boyfriend?"

I open my mouth, about to formulate some sort of explanation, but then: "Don't worry about it," he says, letting me off hook. "I mean, it's no big deal. It's just that I know we got off to a bit of a rough start. Maybe some time when you're free, you'll let me make it up to you. We can grab a cup of coffee or something."

"Yeah," I say, trying to keep the peace, even though I have no real intention of going anywhere with him. Even though just moments ago I was fixated on getting over Ben.

"So, I think my work here is finished." He looks at the table. "Unless there's something else I can help you with?"

"No," I say, following his gaze, noting that even the water cups are symmetrical. "Everything looks pretty perfect."

"I agree," he says. But he isn't looking at the table now. He's looking toward the side of my face. I can feel the weight of his stare.

I glance up to meet his eye, my insides completely rattled. A second later, the door jingles open.

"Greetings, workers," Spencer announces. He's carrying a crate full of molds. "We have a lot of work to do in preparation for Valentine's Day. Nothing says lovin' like boob mugs and penis straws. I need to get these poured, cleaned, and fired, pronto. The group from the senior center will be in next week to work on them. Camelia, can I count on you?"

I nod, relieved when Adam heads back downstairs. It's not that I don't appreciate the fact that he's trying to be nice. I'm just not ready for that kind of niceness—not yet at least.

17

February 23, 1984

Dear Diary,

Mrs. Trigger is fed up with my so-called
morbid art. But I'm fed up with her so-
called brilliant assignments, so I guess
we're even.

What if I don't want to sketch a bowl
full of fruit? What if I want to draw the
image inside my head: my mother lying on
the ground, with a torn bag of groceries
dumped out around her, and a patch of blood
beneath her head?

I tried to draw the fruit. I really did.
But once I started working, I sort of got
sucked into a zone and didn't really think

about the assignment. The next thing I knew, Mrs. Trigger was ringing the bell for critique. I looked around at everybody else's sketch pads with their pretty bowls of fruit.

And then I looked down at mine. At my mother with blood running from her head and pooling onto the sidewalk.

My palms started sweating and I felt my face go white. I think Morgan McCarthy might have noticed, because she gave me a sickened look.

I ripped the sketch right out of the pad and tore it to bits, saying that it didn't come out the way I liked. Mrs. Trigger tried to snatch the remnants, but she only managed to grab my mother's hand, which is ironically more of my mother than I've ever touched.

I know Mrs. Trigger suspects something's off about me. I know she thinks there's something very dark and scary going on inside my brain. And she's right.

Love,
Alexia

18

*A*T HOME LATER, my parents have already
eaten, but my mom has saved me a plate of
chick-un fajitas, made from seitan (or "satan,"
as my dad and I like to call it), ground macadamia nuts,
and pimentos.

"This is a new recipe for me," Mom buzzes. "Let me
know what you think."

"Dee*lish*," I say, followed by a giant gulp of coconut
milk to wash it down.

She slides onto the stool beside me at the kitchen
island. "How was school?"

"Okay, I guess."

"That's it?" She balks. "How was Ben? Is he back?"

I nod, reluctant to tell her anything more, even though
I know she wants the full scoop. My mom has wanted the
full scoop on just about every detail of my life ever since I
was abducted last fall. I know it's because she still feels

guilty about having been out of the loop back then—she never saw anything even remotely as horrific as that coming—but she definitely had her reasons.

I wasn't exactly filling her in on everything that was going on with me at the time—all the weird notes and all the cryptic warnings. But I had my reasons too. Aunt Alexia, my mom's sister, had just tried to commit suicide, and my mom was dealing with drama of her own.

"Did you talk to him?" she asks, still fishing around about Ben.

"Briefly."

"And?"

"And he doesn't really want to see me anymore. He just wants to get on with his life."

"I'm sorry," she says, wrapping her arm around my shoulder. She smells like the inside of her yoga studio—sandalwood incense and candle wax. "But maybe that's for the best. For now, anyway."

I purse my lips, fighting the urge to get emotional all over again.

"Are you okay with his decision?" she asks.

"What do *you* think?"

"I think it takes a lot of courage for him to come back to school. It must be very difficult with a reputation like his. With so many people against him before he even has a chance to open his mouth."

"*I'm* not against him."

"I know. But it still might be a good idea to give him a little space, especially since he's asking."

"You sound like Wes and Kimmie."

"Well, they're pretty smart friends, don't you think?" As she gets up to fix herself a cup of dandelion tea (her surefire cure for tension), I wash my plate off in the sink and snag a couple granola bars for later.

Before I head off to my room, I grab my mail off the kitchen table and then turn to say good night, but Mom isn't paying attention. She sneaks one of her tranquilizer pills and sips it down with her tea, not even noticing that I'm still standing here.

"Mom?"

"Huh?" she says, finally tuning in.

"How's Aunt Alexia doing?"

"Not so great, I guess. She's being transferred to a hospital in Detroit. They have a specialist out there who wants to work with her. . . . She specializes in treating women her age who have suicidal tendencies."

"Don't they have specialists here?"

She takes another sip. "It's nothing for you to worry about."

"But maybe I want to know."

She looks away. "Well, I really don't want to talk about it right now, okay?"

I give a reluctant nod, wondering if this is the kind of thing she opens up about in therapy. After everything that happened last fall, my once chemical-free mom started meeting with a pill-prescribing therapist once a week, though she barely ever mentions it at home.

"Did you have enough to eat, sweetie?" she continues.

"More than enough." I give my stomach a good patting, grateful that she didn't see me throw most of my food away.

"Well, there's plenty more in the fridge if you want a second helping."

"Thanks," I say, then give her a kiss on the cheek.

I tell her good night and head off to bed, part of me feeling guilty for keeping things a secret; another part glad to be sparing her the truth.

$\mathcal{J}$N MY ROOM, I drop my book bag to the floor and sift through my stack of mail. I've been receiving tons of college stuff lately—mostly brochures, postcards, and information packets—thanks to an online survey I filled out.

I open a large padded envelope from the University of Hawaii, trying to picture myself studying on a sandy white beach, a coconut-filled drink in one hand and some exotic fruit in the other. The thought of it makes me smile, and when I think about it, this is probably the first time I've smiled all day.

I take a deep breath and continue through the pile. All of the other schools, regardless of how big their dorm rooms are or how pristine the facilities promise to be, pale in comparison to the hula girl idea now stuck in my head. The idea of me getting far, far away from here.

Finally I reach the last envelope and tear it open. But

instead of the standard letter inviting me to tour the campus, there's a newspaper clipping inside. At first I think it might be some new and innovative marketing tactic to snag my attention, but then I notice it's a clipping from our town's paper.

I turn it over in my hands, suddenly feeling a tunneling sensation inside my chest. It's the article about Debbie Marcus's accident last September. The heading reads "Hit-and-Run Leaves Girl in Coma" and details what happened that night, how a car traveling at least thirty miles per hour knocked Debbie to the ground. A witness—some guy who'd just come out of Finz, the restaurant on Columbus Street—said she fell and hit her head against the pavement. There's a photo of the restaurant beside the article.

I grab the envelope, in search of a return address, but there isn't one, nor is there a postmark. Only my name and address are printed on the front, meaning someone must have dropped this off for me, just like they left those photos in my bedroom. Just like what was happening four months ago when mysterious pictures were left inside my mailbox.

They hadn't been mailed either.

I swallow hard and reach for the phone. At the same moment, the newspaper photo catches my eye again, and I look a little closer.

Above the door of the Finz restaurant sign is a wooden cutout of a swordfish. The swordfish is jumping upward, as though out of the water.

Exactly like my sculpture.

91

I drop the clipping. There's an acidic taste inside my mouth. A second later the phone rings.

"Hello?" I answer.

It's silent at first, but then I hear a high-pitched giggling sound, as if from far away.

"Hello?" I repeat, louder this time, tempted to hang up.

After a few moments, the giggling finally stops. "You'll be next," a voice whispers. It's an angry hisslike tone that nearly makes me drop the receiver.

"Who is this?" I insist. I look toward my window. The curtains are parted, the blind is rolled to the top.

I spring from my bed to tug the blind down.

"You'll end up like her," the voice continues; it's followed by a weird crackling sound.

"Who is this?" I repeat.

But the line is dead.

20

*A*T SCHOOL THE NEXT DAY, I tell Kimmie and Wes all about what happened. We're sitting on the sidelines in gym, all of us having conveniently forgotten our sweatpants and sneakers, and fully prepared to accept our sentence of cleanup duty after school. Some matters just can't wait until lunchtime.

"You seriously couldn't tell if the voice was male or female?" Wes asks.

"Not that it matters," Kimmie sighs. "I mean, with voice-altering software, tone-changing phone devices, and pitch-sensitive voice transformers with reverberation capabilities, I swear, it's like a stalker's paradise."

"Okay, now you're starting to scare me," Wes says.

"No, scary is the way people can alter their voices on cue. Like your imitation of that creepy guy who lives at your house."

"You mean my dad?" He laughs.

"Seriously, it gives me chills just thinking about it," she says.

"But I'm most proud of my Marge Simpson impersonation," he says, making his voice super raspy.

"Still, it's all so vague," she continues. "I mean, 'You'll be next'? 'You'll end up like her'? Couldn't the caller be a bit more specific?"

"They're obviously talking about Ben's ex-girlfriend," I say.

"And why is that obvious?" Wes asks. "They could be talking about Debbie."

"Which, when you think about it, would be a whole lot better," Kimmie says. "I mean, she only ended up in a coma."

As if that's supposed to make me feel better.

Wes gestures to Debbie standing at the sidelines, pretending to play basketball for the blue team, but really doing her best to avoid actually having to participate. "You just never know," he says. "One day a sneeze away from death—"

"The next, just killing the game," Kimmie says of Debbie's less-than-stellar sporting skills.

"I figure the same person who called me is the one who left that newspaper article," I say.

"The same one who left you the snapshots of the shrine and the Ben graffiti," Wes adds.

"Someone's definitely messing with you," Kimmie says, the newspaper clipping pressed between her fingers.

"Yeah, but *why?*" I say, noticing the hole in Kimmie's black lace socks. Mr. Muse ordered us to remove our "wood-dulling" shoes before we stepped out onto the recently painted gym floor. The smell of polyurethane is still thick in the air.

"Maybe the same reason Debbie's friends made it look like she was being stalked," Kimmie says. "People have nothing better to do in this lame-ass town."

I nod, thinking how I said something similar to Adam at the studio yesterday. "Except if this is a joke, it's so far from funny."

"I agree." Wes nods. "I mean, comas, dead-girl shrines, and death threats? It can all be such a downer."

"So what are you going to do?" Kimmie asks me.

I shake my head since I honestly don't know.

"I think you should tell your parents," she says. "Or go to the police."

"Even though Matt's in Louisiana?"

"Wait, is that a rhetorical question?" she asks.

I nibble my lip, wishing I could just talk to Ben about everything, that he would touch my hand, and tell me whether or not I need to be worried. "Maybe you guys are right." I gaze out at Debbie on the court. She stands at the free-throw line, dribbling the ball. The smacking sound of rubber against wood makes my head ache. She finally shoots, but misses.

"Poor girl." Kimmie shakes her head.

"I think she still blames Ben," I say. "You should have seen the way she looked at him in the hallway the other day."

"Didn't someone catch her up to the facts after the coma?" Kimmie asks. "That her dumb-ass friends wanted her to think she was doomed. That *they're* the ones responsible for her so-called stalking."

"Maybe it doesn't matter," I say. "Maybe some people will believe whatever they want, regardless of facts."

"Well, all I know is that when all that drama went down last fall, she *did* go to the police," Wes says. "And look at what happened to her."

"I know," I whisper.

"So maybe you *should* wait," he continues. "I mean, what are you going to tell the police anyway? That first you were hearing voices in your basement? And now someone's pranking your house? They'll give you a straitjacket and then tell you to call them when something big happens."

"Except if I were you," Kimmie says, "I wouldn't wait around for something as big as getting abducted again."

"Agreed," Wes says. "Better to do something *pre*-kidnapping. Maybe right around the time when the stalker in question leaves a dead rodent in your mailbox."

"Not funny," I tell them.

"Who's laughing?" Kimmie's eyes grow wide. The jet-black shadow shading her lids accentuates her pale blue eyes. "I'm really starting to worry about you."

Wes snatches the newspaper clipping from Kimmie and drops it into my lap. "Why not give some of this stuff to Ben and have him touch it?"

"Good idea," Kimmie says.

"But he'll probably refuse," I sigh. "Just like he refused to touch the note I got in the bathroom."

"Because it was sticky?" Wes makes a face.

"Because the note held my energy," I explain, resisting the urge to bean him on the head with one of the runaway basketballs.

"And he'd rather you be in danger than get himself involved?" Kimmie asks.

"Wow, that's harsh," Wes says.

"But it's also obviously true," I say. "Except he doesn't believe I'm in danger. He thinks the note from the bathroom was a joke."

"Have you talked to him about the whole touch-powers-being-transferred possibility?" Kimmie asks.

I nod. "And the answer was negative."

Kimmie shakes her head, clearly disappointed. "So then, how do you explain the swordfish sculpture?"

"Have you been to Finz recently?" Wes asks. "Maybe you saw the swordfish logo and just forgot about it."

I nod again, thinking how it was just a couple nights ago, when I went on that walk with Ben, that we ended up on Columbus Street. Is it possible that the image subconsciously stuck with me somehow?

"Well, seafood aside, you need to do something. And sooner rather than later." Kimmie flares out the skirt of her baby-doll dress and smooths out her leggings, commenting to Wes that his tight black jeans look rather legging-ish as well. "You know I'm all for vintage," she tells him, "but that greaser 1950s look is all wrong for you."

"Thanks, but I've had enough fashion advice from my dad for one day."

"He's not into the James Dean look for you either?"

"He's not into my look *period*. He thinks my hair's too long, my chest's too small, and he's started calling me Wuss instead of Wes, insisting that he needs to buy me a dress to go with my tights."

"Your dad has man-boobs, cankles, and mama-hips," Kimmie snaps. "Who's he to talk about style?"

"Are you still seeing Wendy?" I ask, noticing how Wes's hair does seem a bit longer than usual. Still, he's got it fully encrusted with mousse, per usual, like maybe he's trying to go for that greaser effect after all.

"Wendy dumped me." He sulks. "Two weeks ago. I don't want to talk about it."

"How does someone you pay to pose as your girlfriend dump you?" Kimmie asks.

"I don't want to talk about it," he repeats.

"Well, whatever; your dad's a freak," Kimmie says. "Shall we move on?"

But before we can move too far, Mr. Muse tells us to stop talking completely. "This isn't the cafeteria, ladies," he snaps. "Whiner, you should know better," he says, turning to Wes.

Freshman year, Wes was branded with the name Whiner (short for Wesley, the Oscar Meyer Whiner). It all started when he showed up to the Halloween dance dressed as a six-foot-long wiener. A couple of the lacrosse players swiped his bun, and Wes "whined" to the chaperones, scoring the players a big fat detention, and Wes a very undesirable nickname.

"Socialize on your own time," Mr. Muse continues. "Not mine." He follows up by handing us each a health book: *What's Going on Down There? For Girls and Those Who Love Them.* There's a picture of a prepubescent girl on the front cover, wearing a pink-and-white polka-dot bikini. "I want to see the first three chapters outlined in your notebooks by the end of the block," Muse barks.

"I seriously hate this school," Wes says, once Muse is out of earshot. Instead of taking notes, Wes draws a whip in the hand of the girl on the front cover, and a dog collar around her neck.

21

I SPEND THE NEXT DAY and a half trying to talk to Ben, but he doesn't go to the cafeteria at lunchtime. I don't see him between classes or after school. And he isn't answering my phone calls.

And so all during lab I try to get his attention by looking in his direction, clanking two graduated cylinders together so they make an annoying ping sound, and letting the spine of my book smack down hard against the table. But he doesn't as much as glance up in my direction.

Not once.

While Tate, my new lab partner, orders me to begin chopping up a head of red cabbage (we're doing an experiment that measures the pH levels of a rabbit's favorite food), I watch Ben laugh over something Rena said, and try not to cut my finger.

It seems Ben and Rena already have their cabbage chopped. While Ben, clearly avoiding Rena's touch, reads the directions aloud, she places the perfectly diced cabbage pieces into a beaker and pours hot water over the top.

"The pieces are too big," Tate squawks, referring to my cabbage shreds.

At the same moment, Rena lets out a loud and grating laugh. Ben's eyes crinkle up and his lips spread wide into a smile worthy of a magazine cover. Meanwhile, a fist-size lump forms inside my throat and I seriously want to be sick.

A second later, Tate nabs the knife right out of my hands, completely agitated by my lack of focus. "It was so much better with Rena," he snaps.

But obviously Rena didn't agree.

She and I were lab partners last year in bio. She's one of those students who has to get an A in everything she does, including gym, or else the world, as she knows it, will come crumbling down around her. Her pursuit of perfection is undoubtedly the reason she ditched Tate in the first place. The boy isn't exactly known for his good grades.

While Tate scurries to keep up with the rest of the class, cramming a fistful of barely chopped cabbage leaves into our beaker and dousing water on top of it, I try to redeem myself by taking the lab book and reading him the directions aloud.

"Sharp objects, please," the Sweat-man announces. He moves around the room collecting the numbered knives into a large steel box, muttering something about how the administration insists he keep them under lock and key and for experimental purposes only, even though he has fantasies of alternative uses. "Kidding, of course." He chuckles. "Well, not really."

I give the Sweat-man our knife and then proceed to tell Tate to filter the cabbage material from the beaker, letting the water remain. "The solution should be a red-purple color," I say, peeking out from behind the book to see. But our color is more like muted pink at best.

"What happened?" Tate asks. He gives his straggly ponytail a frustrated tug.

"I don't think we left the water in long enough," I say, rereading the directions. "Was the water steaming when you poured it in?"

Naturally Tate blames me, telling me that I should have said something in advance, that I wasn't paying attention, and that he's already failing chemistry big-time.

"I'm sorry," I say, looking back at Ben and Rena. Their solution is a pretty shade of red that reminds me of valentine roses. They've already got the liquid separated into several glass jars, and they're adding various household products to each—lemon juice, baking soda, vinegar, and antacids—to measure the pH levels.

Rena goes to hand one of the jars to Ben, but he avoids it by jotting something down in his notebook.

"What should we do now?" Tate asks, interrupting my gawking. He pops one of our antacids into his mouth.

I glance at the Sweat-man, wondering if he'll let us start again, but before I can ask, the classroom wall phone rings.

"Mad science," he says, answering the phone. A few seconds' worth of muffled conversation later and the Sweat-man finally hangs up. "Nature calls," he announces. "And so does my wife. This could take a bit, but keep working." He opens the door that adjoins the Spanish classroom next to us, tells Mrs. Lynch that he needs to step out for a few minutes, and then leaves us.

Alone.

I gaze back at Ben. He and Rena look pretty finished with the experiment, each recording their findings in their lab books. They seem to have just about every color of the rainbow going—from red to greenish yellow.

"I'll be right back," I whisper to Tate.

"Wait—*what*? Where are you going?" he barks.

I ignore him and make my way over to Ben and Rena's table.

Rena's mouth twitches, as if my mere presence irritates her. "Can we help you with something?" she asks.

"Ben?" I say, forcing him to look up at me finally.

"We're a little busy," Rena continues.

"It'll just be a second," I say, keeping focused on him. "Then I'll leave you alone. I promise."

Ben studies me for about half a second before turning to Rena: "Would you mind giving us a minute?"

Rena rolls her eyes, indeed appearing to mind, but she gets up anyway, telling me I'm lucky she has to go to the little girls' room.

While she heads off to ask Mrs. Lynch for permission and a hall pass, I slide into the seat beside Ben, noticing how he smells like vanilla. And how he looks like a movie star. His crewneck sweater hugs his chest. His dark gray eyes are wide and intense. And there's a trace of sweat on his brow.

"Is something wrong?" he asks.

I nod and pull the photos from my pocket. Using his and Rena's books as a makeshift barricade so no one else can see, I place the photos down in front of him on the table.

The picture of Julie's shrine.

And the photo of the graffiti.

I see Ben's face fall, and suddenly wish I'd never shown him these pictures.

"I'm sorry," I say, realizing this must be horrible for him.

"What's that?" he asks, noticing the newspaper clipping still wadded up in my hand.

I reluctantly set it down beside the photos. "Someone left these things for me," I explain, keeping my voice low. "Somebody called me, too. They said that I'm next."

"Next *what*?"

"I don't know," I say, my voice barely above a whisper. I flip the shrine photo over so he can see the message scribbled across the back.

"If I didn't know better, I'd almost think this stuff was from me."

"Why *you*?" I ask, remembering how Kimmie suggested the same.

"'Let's go for a hike'?" he reads aloud. "It's almost like

a threat. Like someone wants you to *think* it's me."

"But you have no reason to threaten me."

Ben nods slightly and searches my face. His eyes linger a moment on my lips, but he doesn't exactly dispute the idea. "So, do you have any idea who all this might be from?" he asks.

"I was hoping you could help me."

"Can't this wait until later?"

"If I'll have until later."

Ben lets out a tense sigh and looks around the room. No one's watching. And so he takes the shrine photo and places it on his lap, under the table.

He closes his eyes. His shoulders tremble slightly, as if his hands are shaking too. A few seconds later he gives the photo back. "Nothing," he whispers.

"Nothing?"

He shakes his head and quickly glides his fingers over the graffiti photo and the newspaper clipping. "Just cotton," he says.

"What do you mean?"

"I mean, I just feel you, your clothes, your pants. You must have had this stuff in your pocket for a while. All the original vibe is gone."

"So then, touch *me*," I say, remembering what he told me last fall—how his power is most effective when there's skin-to-skin contact.

I move my hand just inches from his.

"Not now," he says.

"Then when?"

Ben looks back down at the shrine photo. "This isn't a good time," he whispers.

But then he touches me anyway.

His hand skims over mine, causing my insides to bubble and stir. He clasps my fingers ever so gently, like he's still afraid of hurting me.

Don't let go, I want to scream. My whole body aches for him to hold me.

A few moments later, he releases my hand. He opens his eyes and scoots his seat back.

"Well?"

"Nothing," he says, trying to control his breath.

"What do you mean 'nothing'? You didn't feel *anything*?"

"I didn't feel anything dangerous," he says to correct me.

"Then what *did* you feel?" I ask, noting his sweaty face.

"You're supposed to be relieved, by the way," Ben continues, ignoring the question. "This is *good* news. It probably means someone's just trying to mess with you."

I know he's right about a sense of relief, but I can't help feeling disappointed too. I mean, how can he touch me and not feel a thing, when all I have to do is look at him and my entire body quakes?

"Maybe you should try again," I suggest. "You weren't exactly touching me hard."

"I'm sorry if it's not the answer you want to hear."

"I just don't understand," I say, trying to be strong even though every inch of me feels suddenly broken. "How can you feel nothing . . . after *everything*?"

"I'm not exactly feeling anything warm and fuzzy about you either," the Sweat-man says, standing right over me now.

A sprinkling of laughter erupts in the classroom. The Sweat-man continues to poke fun by telling the class about some puppy love he had back in the fifth grade— something about a girl with braids, a candy apple present, and how he'd asked to switch seats too.

Then he rewards me with a big fat detention for abandoning my lab partner. And a big fat zero for our failed pH experiment.

I glance over at Tate, who's obviously given up completely. The poor boy is using a cabbage leaf as a makeshift beret. I get up and take my seat beside him at the front of the room, without another single look in Ben's direction.

22

March 5, 1984

Dear Diary,

Yesterday I had a voice stuck inside my head. It was my mother's, and she was screaming.

At first I thought it was really happening, that she was really yelling out in pain and pleading for help. I stepped out of my bedroom and looked around the house, trying to find her. I even went outside. But she wasn't around, and her car was gone.

I thought I was going crazy, but then Jilly called from the hospital about an hour later, telling me that our mother had slipped on a patch of ice coming out of the grocery store. She'd fallen hard against the pavement, and needed stitches on her scalp.

I hung up the phone, thinking about the sketch I ripped up in Mrs. Trigger's class. Then I cried myself to sleep.

Love,
Alexia

23

*B*Y THE END OF THE SCHOOL DAY, pretty much everyone's heard about what happened in chemistry—that Ben no longer feels anything for me . . . quite literally.

Most people say it's a good thing, joking that if Ben and I were to wind up a couple, my body would probably end up ditched in a shallow grave somewhere.

But I overhear a freshman girl tell her friends the news is tragic. "He saved her life," she reminds them.

Kimmie says the news is neither good *nor* tragic. "You've already heard me lecture you on the merits of moving on, but the fact that Ben abandoned his whole 'no-touch' policy and felt you up in chem lab . . . now *that's* promising. Not to mention hot."

I know she's right about the moving on part, especially since Ben didn't sense anything dangerous when he touched me. Plus I promised him that I'd leave him alone.

And he didn't seem to object.

It's after school, after my double detentions for gym and chemistry, and I'm at Knead, about to begin working on a new piece. I wedge the clay out against my board, enjoying the therapeutic quality of each smack, prod, and punch.

As the clay oozes between my fingers and pastes against my skin, images of all sorts begin to pop into my head. I try my best to push them away, to focus instead on the cold and clammy sensation of the mound and the way it helps me relax. But after only a few short minutes of solitude, I hear someone storm their way up the back stairwell. At first I think it's Spencer, but then I hear the voice:

"I'm coming up the stairs," Adam bellows. "I'm approaching the studio area, about to pass by the sink."

I turn to look, noticing how he's standing only a few feet behind me now.

"I hope I didn't startle you this time," he says.

"Ha-ha." I hold back my smile.

"I would have called your cell to tell you I was coming up, but you never gave me your number."

"I'm fine," I assure him, unable to stifle a giggle.

"So what are you working on?" He looks toward my workboard.

"I don't know yet. I'm having too much fun thwacking to actually sculpt something meaningful."

"Should I be scared?"

I hold the clay mound like a baseball, ready to pitch at

him, but instead I plop it back onto my board.

"I take it you had another rough day?" he asks.

"I already told you; it's been more like a rough year."

"And still you won't let me treat you to coffee." He shakes his head as if the idea of it is appalling. "I poured, pulled, and cleaned all the Valentine's Day stuff, by the way. I think the ladies at the senior center will be pleased."

"Seriously? We're done?"

He nods. "The pieces are in both kilns as we speak."

"Thank you," I say, practically in awe.

"No sweat." He smiles. A dimple forms in his cheek. "I was bored. I've been spending way too much time here."

"And why's that?"

"I could ask *you* the same thing. Isn't this your day off too?"

I shrug and gaze back at my workboard. "Sculpting helps me unwind, I guess. It's sort of my escape."

"Well, I'm escaping too. I have an obnoxious roommate with an even more obnoxious girlfriend. They spend all their time in our apartment, monopolizing the TV, eating all my food, and arguing over who loves the other more. It's really pretty sickening. Plus, Spencer doesn't seem to mind if I hang out here."

"Not if you're getting all the work done."

"Well, I thought I'd be nice and spare you from having to clean boob mugs and penis straws."

"Thanks," I repeat, feeling a smile spread across my face.

"So, is that still a no on the coffee?"

I look away, almost able to hear Kimmie's voice telling me to go, that this doesn't mean I have to marry the guy, and that this is obviously what Ben wants too.

"Come on," he says. "I'll even treat you to a scone."

"Well, when you put it that way, why not?"

24

I SUGGEST TO ADAM that we go to the Press &
Grind, just a few doors down from Knead. Since
neither of us is actually scheduled to work, we
lock up the studio and make our way down there.

The place is fairly deserted, just a few stragglers working on their laptops and a group of ladies knitting. We
order cappuccinos with extra foam, maple-walnut scones,
and then claim the cushy velvet chairs in the corner.

"Wow, this is pretty good," Adam says, taking a sip.
"But I bet it'd even be better out of a boob mug."

"Very funny."

"More like mind-boggling. I mean, who even buys
that stuff?"

"Leave it to Spencer to find the clientele. I think we
must be one of the last remaining pottery shops to still
pour our own slip molds."

"Well, I've been pouring those molds for days." He

flashes me his clay-laden fingernails.

"Do you still like working at Knead?"

"It's cool," he says, wiping his froth mustache with a napkin. "I like how Spencer's so laid-back."

"How did you even know he was hiring?"

"I don't think Spencer even knew it himself. It was a timing thing, really. I was just going around town one day, filling out applications, when I saw Spencer lugging a bunch of boxes out of his truck. I offered to help, and he asked me if I wanted a job."

"That sounds like Spencer," I say.

"Cool, right?"

"Pretty cool. And pretty spontaneous."

"Well, it works for me," he says, taking a bite of scone. "Because I wasn't really into the alternative."

"Which was?"

"Waiting tables at the Jungle Café, the only place I could find that was hiring. You know they make you dress in safari gear, and pretend like you're looking for elephants? It's not exactly good for the self-esteem."

I let out a laugh, nearly choking on a piece of scone. Adam laughs too. And finally I feel like I'm loosening up.

We end up talking about his school plans. He wants to transfer to the Boston School of Architecture in a couple years, and I tell him how I'd like to study in a big city too. "I'm so done with this small-town way of life," I tell him.

"What's so bad about a small town?"

"Where do I even begin?"

"Right." He scratches his chin in thought. "I think

you may have mentioned something about people making up stories because they're bored. I guess I wasn't listening completely. Too distracted that you might tear my head off, I think."

"Sorry."

"No problem," he says, meeting my gaze. "You're making up for it now."

I feel my face get hot, and wonder how to respond. Luckily, I don't have to.

Adam takes another sip and tells me that he's from a small town too. "There were only fifty-two kids in my high-school graduating class. This place is a metropolis as far as I'm concerned."

"Well, I hope you have a good map."

"What for when I've got the best tour guide around? If you're willing, that is."

"Excuse me?"

"What do you say?" He leans forward in his seat. "Do you want to go out sometime?"

"*Out?*"

"Yeah." His brown eyes soften. "You know, like, on a date. I order a mean pepperoni pizza."

"Really?" I say to fill the silence.

"You don't have to answer me now," Adam says. "You can think about it. I'll wait." He sits back in his seat and takes a couple giant bites of scone, polishing it off completely. Then he gulps down the remainder of his cappuccino, commenting on the durability of the foam: "Nice and frothy, just the way I like it." Finally he wipes his mouth, peeks at his watch, and looks back in my direction. "Okay, so time's up. What's the verdict?"

I let out yet another laugh, surprised at how much fun I'm having, and how easily the word *yes* seems to roll right off my tongue.

25

*I*T'S DINNERTIME and I'm not exactly hungry, even when my dad bribes me with a chili cheese burrito at Taco Bell. "We'll tell your mom we're heading out to do an errand at the mall, but instead we'll make a run for the border. What do you say? We can hit the drive-through and eat in the parking lot." He flashes me his pocketful of chewing gum and breath mints. "Essentials," he says with a wink, "to cover our spicy breath afterward."

"A tempting offer," I say, especially considering that Mom's serving up raw-violi for dinner tonight. It's just that there's so much conflicting emotion rolling around inside my head right now that food isn't exactly appealing.

I give Dad a rain check on his offer, and dive into my homework. I'm determined to redeem myself after today's botched chemistry experiment. I'm thinking that maybe if I can fix that, then I can work on the other straggling pieces of my life.

I grab some red cabbage and start to chop it up. Meanwhile Mom, completely ecstatic about the assignment, loads the kitchen island with items from the fridge, telling me she's been meaning to check the acidity of some of her favorite treats. Together we check the pH levels of things like apple juice, coconut milk, brown-rice syrup, and green tea. Then I record my findings, actually excited to show the Sweat-man my results, despite the fact that I've already received a big fat goose egg of a grade.

It just feels really good to fix something.

Later, in bed, I toss and turn, unable to shut my mind off. It's a little after eleven and I can't stop thinking about my day. I had a really fun time with Adam, and yet just being with him—laughing at his jokes and even considering a date—makes me feel like I'm cheating on Ben. I know it makes no sense, and the fact that it doesn't is what's keeping me awake.

I snuggle my stuffed polar bear closer, tempted to give Kimmie a call. I reach for my cell phone and it rings in my hand.

"Hello?" I say, assuming it's her.

"Hey," a male voice says. "It's me."

"Adam?" I ask, not recognizing the number on the caller ID screen.

"Try again."

"Ben?"

"I'm sorry to call so late."

"Where are you calling from?"

"I'm on my aunt's cell. My phone isn't working right."

"Oh," I say, wondering if that's part of the reason why I was having so much trouble reaching him before.

"Were you sleeping?" he asks.

"Not really."

"Yeah, me neither. I guess I kind of just wanted to talk to you about today."

"Okay," I say, completely taken aback.

"It's nothing bad," he continues. "I mean, like I said, I didn't sense anything alarming."

"Then *what?*"

"Do you think that maybe we can talk in person?"

"Right now?"

"Please," he insists. His voice crackles over the word. "I don't think I'll be able to sleep otherwise."

A better part of me wants to tell him no, but instead I mumble a yes, hoping it'll help bring closure to what still feels like a wide-open sore.

We make plans to meet up at the end of my street. There's an all-night diner on the main road. I climb out of bed and pull on my coat, checking the hallway to see if my parents are asleep. They are. Their door is closed and the light's turned off. And so I slip on my boots and climb out the window.

The air is absolutely frigid tonight. Tears run down the sides of my face. I burrow my hands deep in my pockets and move quickly down the road, already able to hear Ben's motorcycle from just a couple streets away.

He pulls up beside me and parks his bike in front of

the diner. "Thanks for coming out," he says, opening the door wide.

We order at the counter—hot chocolates and blueberry muffins—and then take our tray to a table in the corner.

"So, what's going on?" I ask, noticing how sullen Ben looks.

He leans in close, as if what he has to say is really important, but instead he just stares at me. His dark gray eyes are runny from the cold. "I just kind of wanted to see you," he says.

"Oh." I feel my face crinkle in confusion. "I thought it was something urgent."

"Who's Adam?"

"Is that why you wanted to see me?"

"I'm just curious." He shrugs. "You said his name when I called you."

I'm tempted to tell him that he no longer has any right to ask about other guys, but instead I just say: "He's someone I work with."

"And you're seeing him?"

"I thought you said you wanted space."

"I do."

"Then what are we doing here?"

A second later, a waitress comes to check on us. "Is everything okay?" she asks, noticing that neither of us has touched our food.

I nod slightly, and she turns away.

Meanwhile, Ben continues to study my face. "We're

here because you said something today that bothered me."

"What?" I ask, wishing he'd just spit it out.

He bites his lip and gazes at my mouth, afraid to tell me, maybe. But then he finally says it: "When you said that if I'd help you, you'd leave me alone."

"You don't want that?"

"You don't have to leave me alone completely. It's not like we can't talk sometimes."

"Isn't it? I mean, we've already been through this. I can't be with you if I'm not allowed to touch you. If I'm not allowed to feel what I'm feeling."

"And what *are* you feeling?"

I shake my head, refusing to open up again. "I can't do this. I can't be all vulnerable, only to have you change your mind five minutes later. You said you wanted space and so I'm giving it to you. I'm trying to move on."

"It seems like you've already moved on."

I shake my head, fighting the urge to tell him that there's nothing going on between Adam and me. Because he honestly has no right to know. "Maybe we should leave," I say, sliding my chair back.

"Not yet."

"Do you have something else to tell me?"

He opens his mouth as if to speak, but instead he touches me. He slides his hand across the table and rests it on my forearm.

"What are you doing?" I whisper, but I'm not sure the words are audible.

Ben clenches harder until my arm stings, and I almost have to tug away.

"What are you feeling for?" I ask, fully aware that he's trying to read me. At first I assume it's because of everything that's been going on—the photos, the notes, the phone call.

But then it hits me: he already said I was safe. He said he didn't sense anything dangerous when he touched me before. And so far, all it seems he's wanted to know about is Adam.

I pull away and stand from the table. "I have to go."

"Please, Camelia, no."

"I'm sorry," I say. Tears well up in my eyes. "I can't do this. You can't have it both ways." I turn away, leaving him alone.

26

*I*N MY ROOM I tear off my coat, kick my boots to the corner, and slip into bed, somehow still able to feel Ben's touch on my forearm. I close my eyes and tell myself that I did the right thing.

Even though it hurts like hell.

Even though there's a gnawing ache inside me that gets bigger with each breath.

I roll over and bury my face in the covers, trying to think of something, *anything* else: work, school, Kimmie, my mom. . . . But all my thoughts travel back to the same place. Back to him, to how sullen he looked tonight, to the vulnerable gape of his eyes, and everything he said. It was almost as if something between us had died.

Or maybe together we're killing it off.

I listen hard for the sound of his motorcycle, but the windows are closed and my CD player sings in my ear— the sound of water trickling down a brook. I switched it on to drown out my thoughts. It obviously isn't working.

I toss in bed, noticing how my skin itches and my body feels suddenly sweaty. I sit up finally and reach for my glass of water.

That's when I see him, just a second away from rapping on my window. His face is illuminated by the moon, making him look straight out of a dream.

I open the window wide.

"Take your promise back," he says, before I can utter a single word. "I don't want you to leave me alone."

"I have to."

Ben looks away so that I won't see his eyes tearing up. "I know," he mouths; the words don't come out. "I was just thinking that maybe . . ." He looks at me again, his eyes full of sadness. "We could just be together one last time?"

I know I should say no. For five full seconds I tell myself that I can't possibly allow this to happen. But instead I open the window wider and invite him to crawl inside.

We lie together on the bed, under the covers, and face the window. The moon casts its glow over the mound of our bodies.

I close my eyes and feel Ben's hand slide up my back, underneath my shirt, sending tingles all over my skin. His fingers glide across my shoulders and down my spine, nearly stealing my breath.

And stealing his breath too.

As I start to fall asleep, I hear his breath heaving in and

out. A gasp escapes his throat and he has to pull away, only to do it all over again a few moments later.

At one point in the night, I think I feel his kisses at the nape of my neck, his leg against my thigh, and his body spooning me up from behind.

My blood stirs and my body churns.

But maybe it's all just a dream.

When I wake up the following morning to the buzz of my alarm, Ben is no longer there. A note rests in his place. In bright red cursive, it says "Thanks for breaking your promise and giving me one more night."

I take it and press it against my chest, wishing it were so much more than one night, but grateful just the same. Because maybe this was the closure I was waiting for.

And maybe I'm finally ready to move on.

27

$\mathcal{T}$HE NEXT FULL WEEK goes by in a blur, pretty uneventful and utterly depressing. You'd think that a bit of peace would come as a welcome blessing, but it only affirms the empty sensation inside me—a deep and bottomless pit that I can't seem to fill with food, the company of friends, or even by doing pottery. I feel like one of those windup robots, wired to waddle through life, blindly bumping into walls and colliding with other objects.

That's how out of it I've been.

I haven't really spoken to Ben since that night. Whenever I see him in school we mostly just exchange a nod in passing, or sometimes a faint smile.

Kimmie calls our situation tragically romantic. "You have to admit, it's totally hot of him to give up his own lustful needs because he's afraid he might hurt you. I mean, aside from the other night, that is. He was obviously jonesing for you big-time to pay a visit to your bedroom. And that, my friend, makes him just beastly enough to score huge on my hot-o-meter."

"Beastly?"

"You heard me. A sexy little blending of primal need and old-fashioned chivalry."

"Too bad I'm going out with Adam," I say, opening my closet door wide. Kimmie, my stylist-on-demand, is helping me pick out an outfit for tonight's date.

"Why is it too bad?" She pulls a tube skirt from the rack. "I mean, look at what happened after just one measly scone and cup of coffee with Adam. You scored a date and laughed for the first time in months."

"Not *months*," I correct her.

"Well, whatever, my point is that the possibilities are endless . . . just like Ms. Mazur's ass. I mean, did you see her in pottery class today . . . pink spandex with a T-shirt that barely covered her navel? They should make Spanx a requirement for some outfits."

"Let's leave Ms. Mazur's ass out of this, shall we? Having endless possibilities, as you say, is not the reason I agreed to go on this date. I was hoping that going through the motions of moving on might trick my mind into believing that I am."

"Right," Kimmie says, eyeing a chain-link belt. "It's a win-win. Plus, don't even get me started on my whole Ben-the-stalker-boy theory."

"Because I've heard it already?"

"Well, you have to admit," she says, tossing a

cream-colored cable-knit sweater at me, "leaving you twisted little notes and super-creepy photos would sure be an interesting way to keep you close, but not *too* close."

"Wait, I thought you believed he was stalking me to keep me away, because he wanted me to see him as a killer."

Kimmie taps her chin in thought. "I guess my theory works both ways, doesn't it?"

"Whatever," I sigh. "Let's just hope the stalking stuff has finally stopped. Nothing weird has happened lately."

"Right, because Ben's back to being all 'we need space' again. Just wait till he gets lonely. You'll probably get a pound of chicken thighs or a photo of Julie's headstone in the mail."

"That's sick."

"But possible." She hands me a pair of black tights. "Here. Try all this on for me."

"Fine," I say, refusing to entertain her so-called theories for even one more solitary second.

"Seriously?" Kimmie giggles, holding up a short pleated skirt from the back of my closet. "You've obviously been holding out on me."

"It's from my middle school uniform," I explain, all but yakking over the blue-and-green plaid. "It's sort of sentimental, which is why I keep it."

"This is just the sort of thing my dad wants my mom to wear," she says, checking the size. "The poor woman's barely hanging on to him by a Lee Press-on Nail."

"Kimmie, I'm sorry."

"Whatever." She shrugs, returning the skirt to my closet. "I really don't feel like talking about it right now. Back to happier topics?"

"Gladly," I say, slipping on the tube skirt and sweater, and then yanking on my tights.

"Sexy lady," Kimmie coos. "So where will Adam be taking us this evening?"

"*Us?*"

"Kidding," she says, standing at my dresser mirror. She combs through the jet black layers of her pixie cut, examining the roots, where her natural shade of brown is starting to make an appearance. "Of course, you never know." She meets my eyes in the mirror's reflection. "Maybe I'll show up anyway and stalk you from afar."

"Very funny."

But Kimmie isn't laughing. Instead she flops back on my bed and snuggles Mr. Polar Bear.

28

*I*T'S A LITTLE BEFORE SEVEN when the doorbell rings. I'm thinking it's Adam, but since my parents don't call for me, I finish getting ready. Kimmie has already left. She ran out in a hurry, claiming to have a hot date of her own. Tonight's her first time out with Todd McCaffrey, Debbie Marcus's ex.

"I'll call you as soon as I get in," she promised on her way out. "We'll compare all the sordid details."

"Except mine won't be sordid," I told her.

I still feel conflicted about my date with Adam, but at about quarter past the hour, I head out to the living room, wondering what's keeping him, surprised to discover that he's already here.

He's sitting with my dad, engrossed in conversation. Dad's showing him his high-school yearbook, which is never a good sign.

"How come you didn't tell me that Adam plays

soccer?" Dad asks, spotting me in the doorway.

"Because I didn't know?"

"I *used* to play," Adam corrects, giving me a wink.

"Aw, once it's in the blood, you can never give it up," Dad says. "I used to play offense in high school. In college it was striker, then halfback. "I've got more photos somewhere—"

"We should probably get going," I say, in an effort to save Adam.

"Oh," Dad says, visibly crushed. He closes up his yearbook and hugs it against his chest.

I kiss Dad good-bye, but it doesn't ease his sulking, even when Adam promises to look at his pictures next time.

Finally we leave and Adam opens up the door of his Ford Bronco for me. "It's vintage," he says, pointing out the hubcaps and the shiny new turquoise body. "From the '70s. I restored it myself."

"Nice," I say, sinking into the creamy white vinyl seat.

"I've got the whole evening planned out," he continues, scooting in behind the wheel. "I hope you're ready for some fun." He takes us to the fondue restaurant in the next town over.

"This looks amazing," I say, noticing how the dining area is decorated with rich shades of purple, dangling chandeliers, and French impressionist art. We order sourdough bread chunks with cheddar cheese goo.

"I'm really glad you agreed to come out," he says. "You

were so standoffish at first. I thought maybe you had a boyfriend."

"Well, we sort of just broke up," I say, taking a nervous bite.

"When?"

"Four months ago."

"So you didn't *just* break up," he says. "I mean, it didn't just happen yesterday."

"I guess not." I reload my skewer with some bread. "I guess I was just kind of waiting for him to come back after some time away."

"And did he? Come back, I mean?"

I nod, feeling my neck get hot, wishing we could talk about something else. I take a sip of water and gaze at one of the chandeliers, about to comment on the dangling crystal chunks, but before I can, Adam probes deeper: "So, what happened after he got back?"

"He didn't want to work things out," I say, then take another sip.

"Gotcha," Adam says. "Obviously the guy's an idiot."

"Whatever." I resist the urge to smirk. "It's over. I'm here."

"Well, cheers to that." Adam raises his water glass to clink against mine. Then he proceeds to tell me how his last girlfriend broke up with him because she didn't like his haircut. "Seriously, she couldn't even look at me. She said it made my forehead look extra big and my eyes bug out of my face. I think she compared me to a housefly, but with uglier legs, like a gnat. I guess she picked on my body a lot too. She said I was too wiry . . . like a spider."

"That's crazy," I say, trying not to giggle at the image. I mean, Adam is perfectly good-looking, with a perfectly normal physique.

"I guess she prefers the rocker type," Adam continues.

"Either that or sexier insects."

Adam laughs, and we end up spending almost four full hours at the restaurant, through two more servings of fondue—one made with chicken stock and another with dark chocolate for dessert. Adam talks about his dream of opening up his own architectural design firm one day, and I tell him that I'd love to have my own studio.

"Like Knead?" he asks.

"Maybe, but without the boob mugs."

"Right, better to just have the penis straws."

I let out a laugh, and it's a full ten minutes before either one of us can contain ourselves to talk seriously again.

"I'd love to teach classes without the cookie-cutter molds," I say finally. "I mean, how cool would it be to have an entire class devoted to form, texture, and shape, without having to worry about creating something specific right away?"

"Is that how you were taught?"

I shake my head. "I used to be all about the end product, but I've since learned that sometimes the process is just as important."

"If not more so," Adam says. "It's the journey that makes things interesting, right? So, here's to interesting journeys." He lifts his glass again to clink against mine, and it suddenly occurs to me that I haven't thought about Ben in the last sixty minutes. And that this is the most fun I've had in a really long time.

29

*W*HEN I GET HOME from my date with Adam, my parents are waiting up for me in the living room.

"You're lucky," Dad says, locking the dead bolt behind me. "You made your curfew with three minutes to spare. Your mother was a speed dial away from calling your cell."

"Did you have a nice time?" she asks, blowing out an aromatherapy candle.

"It was fun."

"And that's it?" she asks. "Where is he from? What do his parents do? Does he live in a dorm?"

"Can't this inquisition wait until tomorrow?"

"Not really." Mom rises from the sofa. "You're dating this boy; I want to know about him."

"He was a perfect gentleman," I say to assure her.

"Well that's a relief." She softens finally. "I think it would have broken your dad's heart if you hadn't enjoyed yourself."

"No pressure, of course," Dad says. "You don't have to marry him or anything . . . even though he *was* the lead striker on his high school team for three years in a row."

"I'm going to bed," I say, eager to call Kimmie. I kiss them both good night, and head off to my room.

Kimmie picks up on the first ring: "I want every detail."

"So much for a hello."

"Hello . . . I want every detail."

I give her the CliffNotes version of my date, telling her everything we talked about, and how the food was amazing.

"And *after* the food and talking?" she asks.

"What do you mean?"

"Do I need to draw you a picture?"

"We said good-bye. He dropped me off in front of my house. Then he drove away once I went in."

"And that's it? No smooching? No petting? Not a single brush against the thigh?"

"I'm nowhere near ready for any of the above," I say.

"Unless it's with a certain touch boy, am I right? Did Adam even *try* to go in for a kiss?"

"Nope."

"Which could only mean one thing."

"He's not interested?"

"Even worse," she says. "He must really respect you."

"The horror of it all."

Kimmie laughs and then tells me about her date with Todd. "We went to Pizza Slut and then made out in the parking lot for two hours straight."

"Seriously?"

"I have the hickeys to prove it. I came home tonight totally exposing a really mean-looking one on my neck, but my mom was too engrossed in her Lifetime movie to notice, and my dad still isn't home."

"Oh," I say, glancing at the clock. It's a little after midnight.

"He's been working into the wee hours of the morning," she says, as though reading my mind. "He has a lot of clients in from out of town and he's forced to take them out to dinner and stuff. Not that it would matter. I could probably come home nine months pregnant and neither of them would notice."

"But let's not go testing that theory," I say.

"Are you kidding? I'd have to design a whole new wardrobe. Plus, I hear that feet swell when you're pregnant. Just try to find a pair of vintage heels in a size thirteen."

"Well, that's a relief . . . about the pregnancy thing, I mean."

"Speaking of relief, Todd's completely ecstatic not to be dating Debbie anymore. You were right, by the way, she totally still blames Ben for her stint in coma-ville, hence the evil look she gave him last week."

"Even though it was her friends who were playing a joke on her? Making her all paranoid, making her believe that she was being stalked. . . ?"

"What do you want from me? It's just what Todd said. He also said I have a really pretty mouth. Do you think he was just sucking up?"

"It sounds like he was sucking pretty hard," I say, referring to her hickeys.

"Well, whatever. He said Debbie and him still talk sometimes, since they both live on the same street. Apparently she thinks that if it wasn't for Ben and his seedy past, and coming to our school, nothing like that would ever have happened."

"Now, why doesn't that surprise me?"

"Well, what *might* come as a surprise is the fact that Debbie hasn't ruled out the possibility that Ben's the one who hit her that night."

"He doesn't have a car."

"Yeah, but he doesn't have an alibi either."

"He was with *me* that night," I snap. It's true that he was. That was the night Ben and I ended up at Knead—the night when we first kissed.

"I knew this would make you upset," Kimmie says. "I shouldn't have even said anything."

"No," I insist. "I want to hear it."

"Okay, well, Debbie still argues that Ben would have had enough time to drop you off and then plow her down, because Columbus Street is right near your house."

"And the no-car factor? I mean, the witness was sure it was a car. He even knew the make and model."

"I suppose it doesn't help that they never found the driver, or the car itself."

"You're right," I whisper. "It doesn't help." It's the one tiny detail that's bothered me all along.

30

March 27, 1984

Dear Diary,

My sister announced tonight that she's becoming a vegetarian. Our mother wasn't happy, especially since she made bacon and eggs for supper. At first she told Jilly to just skip the bacon (she'd use it in sandwiches tomorrow), but then Jilly said that she was anti-eggs too, which basically caused our mother to flip out. She threw the frying pan on the floor, told Jilly how ungrateful she is, and then stormed away, slamming her bedroom door behind her.

Jilly gave me her plate full of food so I

wouldn't have to pick mine off the floor.
She fixed herself a bowl of dry cereal.

And then she smiled at me.

It was a knowing smile, as if maybe this
was her way of helping me out, causing
problems to get our mother off my back
for a change, and onto hers.

I smiled back, desperate to ask her if
that was the case, but instead I just
stayed quiet, afraid that I might have
been wrong. If I was wrong, I didn't want to
know it.

Love,
Alexia

31

J WAKE UP EARLY the following morning with an insatiable need to sculpt. It's what I dreamed about all night—until the sun finally peeped in through the cracks of my window shades, nudging me to get up, to go down into the basement studio, and to feel the sticky wet earth against my fingertips.

Barely 9 a.m., my parents have already been up for hours. My mom usually does her sun salutations at 5 o'clock every morning. And Dad hits his NordicTrack around 7. Neither of them is home now, though. They've left a note on the fridge for me, saying they went to Raw for breakfast. And so I grab a quick bowl of sugarcoated cereal from Dad's secret stash and head downstairs.

It's freezing in the basement. It seems my dad left the corner window open a crack to diminish the pottery fumes he insists are real. I close it up, surprised by the strength of the wind; it blows my hair back and makes my eyes water. Still, despite the cold, the sun pours in through the glass, illuminating my worktable. I light one of my mom's aromatherapy candles—one with bits of rose petals embedded into the wax—and inhale the tealike scent.

The clay is cool and moist in my grip. I wedge it out against my board while images of all sorts rush through my brain. I breathe through the sensation, and through the spinning feeling inside my head, trying my best to concentrate on the one image that seems to stand out against all the others. And then I begin to sculpt.

Keeping my clay thoroughly saturated with a sopping-wet sponge, I smooth my fingers over the mound, sealing up cracks and creating arches where I feel they belong. After well over an hour, the clay still doesn't look anything like the picture inside my head. Still, I keep working, trying not to focus so much on the end product, but on the muscles of my hands as they form curves along the base.

I close my eyes again, concentrating on the image I see: a horse, its legs kicked upward as if in a jump. After several more minutes I begin to feel the head appear as I sculpt the mane. I open my eyes, feeling a flood of excitement wash over my skin, just knowing I'm getting things right.

A second later, I hear something behind me. A high-pitched whispering sound.

I stop. I peer around the basement, wondering if it was just my imagination because I know I'm alone. I listen for several more seconds, but between the wind howling outside, causing the house to settle in a series of cracks and hisses, and the perpetual pop and hum of the heating furnace, I can't really tell.

I turn back around to resume my work. A few moments later, I hear it again—only it's clearer this time: "Camelia," a female voice whispers. It's followed by a giggling sound, sending chills straight down my spine.

I blow out the candle and move toward the staircase. "Mom?" I call, wondering if my parents are home from breakfast. But the door that leads upstairs is still closed.

I start up the staircase, noticing the creaking sound beneath my feet. I edge the door open and enter the kitchen. Everything appears normal, just as I left it. But then I hear something else. The windows in the living room rattle from the whipping of the wind outside. I check to make sure the panes are locked, and then continue around the house. The front and back doors are closed and dead bolted. The driveway's empty. And my bedroom looks exactly as I left it.

I reluctantly head back downstairs and switch on the overhead lights. Everything appears just as it should: Dad's tool bench to the left, my sculpture studio just behind it, and all our storage to the right.

So why do I feel like I'm being watched?

I pull my sweatshirt sleeves down over my fingers in an effort to stifle the chill. Then I look back over my shoulder toward the upstairs door, wondering if I should call someone.

Instead I count to ten, reminding myself that I'm alone, that the house is locked, and that Matt is far, far away. Still, I gaze over at the basement windows, wondering if maybe the voice wasn't part of my imagination at all—if maybe it was coming from outside somehow.

I move across the concrete floor, peeking behind old furniture and picking through boxes, until I reach the basement door—the one that leads to the bulkhead that opens to outside. I press my back against it, fighting the urge not to scream.

I mean, am I really hearing voices? Or is it all just in my head?

The image of the horse still alive in my mind, I move toward my studio, hoping my piece didn't get too dry, that I'll still be able to continue my work.

But then I hear more whispering: "Be careful," a voice says, in a piercing tone that vibrates through the center of my gut. It's followed by more giggling.

I reach for my cell phone, realizing it isn't in my pocket. It's upstairs. I survey the room, but I don't see anyone. And everything remains still.

"Who's there?" I call. There's an icy sensation inside my veins.

When no one answers, I take a deep breath and try not to cry, wondering if maybe the answer lies in my sculpture. Maybe I need to complete the piece to understand what the voice is warning me about.

I place my hands over the clay mound. At the same moment, a foreboding feeling settles on my shoulders, making the hairs on the back of my neck stand on end.

"Be careful," the voice whispers again.

I clench my jaw, fighting the urge to cover my ears, even though I end up doing it anyway. My clay-stained hands slide against the sides of my face, over my ears, and I shake my head. "No!" I shout, when the whispering doesn't stop.

I look back over my shoulder, toward the basement door that leads outside. It sounds like the giggling is coming from just behind it. I grab an X-Acto knife from my tray of tools and move back in that direction. My legs quiver with each step. The closer I get to the door, the louder the giggling sound becomes. My heart stomps. Tears soak my cheeks.

The basement door's only inches away; I reach for the knob. In one quick motion, I whisk the door open, the knife held high above my head.

No one's there. There's only a set of steps leading up to the bulkhead door. Still the whispering continues. It's just a faint, faraway voice now, too distant to make out the words.

I climb the steps and unlatch the lever that opens the bulkhead. I swing the doors open wide. Cobwebs fall, brushing against my face, landing on my lips. I wipe them away as best I can and climb outside.

My yard appears absolutely normal with its small brick patio and large grassy area. A tall wooden fence surrounds it. I pace the length, looking for footsteps in the patches of snow, but I don't see anything. And I no longer hear the voice.

I sit down on the edge of a bench and bury my face in

my hands, almost wishing someone *were* out here. At least it would explain the voices.

I wipe my eyes, gearing myself up to go back inside. I'm just about to climb through the doors, when I notice a streak of red down the side of the bulkhead. It looks like paint.

I grab the edge of the door on the right and flip it closed. Someone's written on it. The letters RE are stacked atop the letters AD in a dark red color.

For just a moment I think it's a message directing me to read something. But then I flip the opposite door closed and the message becomes clear: YOU'RE DEAD.

32

EARS FILL MY EYES. I reach out to touch the lettering, wondering if it's still wet, but it's dry—except where droplets of snow have landed over some of the letters, making them look like dripping blood.

I dip my finger into the snow and press down against more of the paint. A smear of red bleeds against my thumb.

I take a step back, slightly startled when I hear a car door slam. I rush to the gate and look out toward the street. It's my parents.

I hurry back inside the house, lock the basement door, and scramble up the stairs before they even make it in.

"Hey, there," Mom says, coming into the kitchen. "Did you find the banana soufflé for breakfast? I should have mentioned it on the note. I just made it this morning, but your dad had a hankering for rawaffles."

"Pronounced rawfuls, taste more like awfuls; translation: raw waffles, made with dehydrated fruit and nuts."

Dad peels off his coat and tosses it on the island. "I had a hankering for fat-laden French toast sopping with maple syrup and melted butter. I mean, who are they kidding with those tasteless disks?"

"Well, excuse me for looking out for your health," Mom says. "Why don't you just go ingest a tub of lard mixed with sugar and chewing tobacco?"

"It'd probably taste better than those rawaffles."

"We need to talk," I say, still trying to catch my breath.

"You bet we do," he says. "I'm so tired of eating chicken feed and bird food."

"Oh, God," Mom says, checking her cell phone messages. Her hand clasps over her mouth.

"What now?" Dad asks.

"It's Alexia," she says. "Her psychiatrist wants to schedule a meeting with the three of us."

"The three of us? As in you, me, and Dad?"

"No." She closes up her phone. "A meeting with Aunt Alexia, the psychiatrist, and me."

"So, that's a good thing, right?" I ask.

"Right," she says, staring off into space.

Dad goes and wraps his arms around her from behind, telling her everything will be fine. "It'll be therapeutic for the both of you," he says.

But my mother appears less than convinced and ends up swatting him away. She absentmindedly opens the fridge, takes out a jar of almond butter, and begins to feed her funk. Meanwhile, I wipe a clay smear from the side of my face, not really knowing what to say. Or what to do.

I end up sneaking off downstairs to cover my horse-in-progress with a giant piece of plastic. Then I dress in layers and head out on the longest walk I can manage, considering the frigid temperature outside.

After a good hour-and-ten minute hike, I find myself at Kimmie's house. She pulls me inside and leads me upstairs while her parents continue to fight in the living room.

"Don't mind the drama," she says, closing her bedroom door behind us. "They've been going at it since last night. Something about him feeling suffocated and my mom's obsessive need to control. I don't know. I sort of lost track around the time he called her a puppeteer and himself a Raggedy Andy doll."

"Kimmie, I'm sorry. What can I do?"

"Turn the music up, will you?" She nods toward her iPod.

I do, and then plop down opposite her on the bed. She's wearing a V-neck sweater that exposes a couple of grape-size hickeys on her neck.

"So, I'm assuming you didn't come here to listen to my parents fighting," she says.

"Who cares why I came? I mean, this can't be easy for you."

Kimmie shrugs and avoids my gaze, but I can see that the fighting clearly affects her. Her eyes fill slightly and a stray tear falls over the black-lined rim. "My dad finally noticed my neck, by the way. But instead of calling for one of our sit-down family powwows, he told my mother she raised a slut. I think that's what spurred the fighting."

"You can't blame yourself."

"Whatever," she says, trying to be tough, even though more tears slide down her cheeks.

I reach out to hug her, allowing her to fall into my embrace, and almost forgetting the reason why I came here in the first place. *Almost.*

A second later there's a knock on her bedroom door. "Who is it?" she shouts in an angry tone that, like the hickeys, I barely recognize on her.

"It's Nate," her brother says. "Can I come in there with you guys? I won't bother you or make any noise."

She doesn't tell him to bug off—something I'd normally expect from her. Instead she invites him in.

"Maybe we should all go someplace," I suggest, able to hear her parents arguing just as soon as the door cracks open.

Nate perks right up, suggesting the ice-cream shop, the movies, or the arcade at the mall.

"I vote we go to Brain Freeze," Kimmie says, checking her vintage Gucci change purse for money. "Therapy in the form of ice-cream sundaes and banana floats."

"I second it!" Nate roars.

"Even though it's fifty below?"

"Suck it up, Chameleon. It's barely a five-minute walk. Plus, who couldn't use a little ice-cream therapy right about now?"

"I could," I admit.

151

"Exactly," she says, flipping her cell phone open. And before I can even say peanut butter barrel with extra whipped cream, Kimmie calls Wes and invites him to come along too.

ES IS ALREADY WAITING for us at Brain Freeze when we arrive. "I didn't know it was 'kids eat free' day," Wes jokes.

"Don't worry about Nate," Kimmie says. "He's already agreed not to make direct eye contact with anyone, and not to do or say anything embarrassing."

"Leave the embarrassing stuff to me," Wes says, snagging a can of whipped cream from the counter and spraying nipples onto his ski vest. "Yummy, Mommy. Come to Papa." He charges at Kimmie, chest-first.

Kimmie lets out a laugh, dodging his creamy nipples. Meanwhile, I step up to the counter and order Nate and me mini peanut butter barrels with extra fudge sauce.

"This is so much more pleasant than listening to my parents try to off each other," Kimmie says as we all slide into a booth at the far corner.

"Details, please," Wes says, digging into what

appears to be a strawberry blitz.

"Later." She motions toward the top of Nate's head.

"I've got details," I offer.

"Thank goodness," Kimmie says, tightening the scarf around her neck, the print of which is oddly apropos—lipstick kisses—to camouflage all her hickeys. "Let's talk about something other than my dysfunctional life."

"Like *my* dysfunctional life," I continue.

"Here," Kimmie says to Nate, emptying out her change purse. "Go play a few rounds of pinball on me."

Nate happily complies, and finally we can get down to business. I proceed to tell them about what happened this morning with the bulkhead message.

"And you waited until now to tell me this?" Kimmie asks.

"There's more to it." I tell them about the voice I heard, followed by the giggling.

Wes perks up. "A female voice?"

"Wait," Kimmie says. "If the whispering was coming from outside, how could you possibly have heard it? Sound travels, but not like that. I mean, through a basement door *and* a bulkhead?"

"Unless this person's a ventriloquist," Wes says, tapping his chin in thought.

"Be serious," she sighs.

"I *am* serious. Didn't you guys see that movie . . . *When a Stranger Calls Back*? The babysitter thought the psycho-in-question was outside, talking to her through the front door, but in fact he was already in the house. Turned out he could throw his voice on cue."

"Okay, getting back to reality," Kimmie says, rolling her eyes. "If someone had only recently painted that message on the bulkhead, don't you think the writing would still have been wet?"

"Exactly," I say, thinking how droplets of snow had dripped down over the letters. "But it also could have been marker. It was really hard to tell."

"Yeah, but even marker would still be wet, right?" she asks. "I mean, considering it was done on metal. . . ."

"Not if it was *permanent* marker," Wes says. "Like a Sharpie. Trust me; that stuff dries instantly. But if the writing was streaky in places, as you say, then they probably used something else. Your best bet is to have a pro take a peek at it."

"Or she could simply have you look at it," Kimmie says to him.

"For all I know, that writing could have been there for weeks," I say.

"Or at least since the last time your parents were in the backyard," Kimmie corrects.

"Which was probably over a month ago for my mom." I gaze at my thumb, where there's still a smear of red. "When it's as cold as ice out, she only ventures as far as the driveway to get into her preheated car."

"Don't you mean as cold as *ass*?" Wes says. "Or at least as cold as *my* ass? This place obviously doesn't believe in turning on the heat. I'm starting to get frostbite." He zips his vest all the way up and peers over his shoulder to give the guy working behind the counter a dirty look.

"You *are* eating ice cream in January," Kimmie reminds him.

"Anyway," I say, getting us back on track. "Let's just say for the sake of argument that the writing was done days, weeks, or even months ago; how do you explain the whole mysterious voice issue?"

"No one was upstairs or in the basement—" Wes begins.

"The TV was off, and so was the radio," Kimmie finishes.

"I know," I repeat. "It doesn't make any sense."

"So you're hearing voices," Wes says, sloughing it off with a wave of his spoon. "It could be a whole lot worse."

"Right," Kimmie says. "Your parents could be trying to rip each other's heads off on a regular basis."

"Or your dad could be calling you 'Wuss,'" Wes says. "And signing you up for Girl Scouts. Did I mention he had a troop leader call my house to ask if I wanted to sell cookies?"

"Bottom line," Kimmie says, "you need to talk to Ben again. You need to tell him about the voices you've been hearing."

"No." I shake my head. "I'm done with Ben. I'm going to give him his space."

"Don't you think he'd want to know if something funky was going on with you?"

I shrug, not quite sure of the answer.

"Did you happen to notice graffiti on any of the other houses in your neighborhood?" Wes asks. "People usually tag in sprees."

"Oh, do they now?" Kimmie raises an eyebrow. "Are we suddenly an authority on defamation?"

"I'm an authority on a lot of things." He licks his spoon clean.

"I need to do more research on psychometry," I say.

"Exactly." Wes nods. "You need to learn all you can so you can start putting this touch talent to good use."

"Which does not include trying to score you a date with someone who doesn't charge an hourly fee," Kimmie says to him.

"Ha-ha." He fakes a laugh.

"You realize that at this point, you have to tell your parents," Kimmie says. "I mean, it's not like they're not going to find out on their own anyway."

"I almost told them this morning."

"But?" she asks.

"But it's complicated," I say, thinking about Aunt Alexia.

"Well, I, for one, am not going to have this hanging over my head," she says. "Either you tell them, or I will. How's that for uncomplicated?"

"I'm all out of money," Nate says, returning to the table.

"And I'm all out of ice cream." Wes pillages from my peanut butter barrel. "What do you say we swing by your place to put an end to the whole paint versus marker mystery?"

"I'm game," Kimmie says. "God knows, checking out deathly stalker messages is a whole lot more fun than being at home."

34

*W*ES PARKS DOWN THE STREET from my house, saying that he doesn't want any parental interference while he investigates the bulkhead. Before getting out of the car, he opens up his glove compartment and pulls forth a magnifying glass, a pair of rubber gloves, and a bottle of nail polish remover.

"Should I be concerned?" Kimmie asks him.

"Just basic staples," he says with an evil grin, "if you want to do things right."

"I do," I assure him.

"Then let's get to work." He pulls the rubber gloves on with a snap.

I lead them down the street, toward my house. Both my parents' cars are parked in the driveway, so I know they're still home. We sneak around the side, by the garage, and scurry through the gate that leads us to the back.

"I'm scared," Nate whispers to Kimmie, trying to keep up.

"Relax," she tells him. "It's broad daylight, in case you hadn't noticed."

"Which is why we're not wearing black," Wes explains. "Best to skulk in street clothes during the day."

"Like you could ever blend in in a get-up like that." She gestures to his bright yellow parka and army-green snow boots.

Once in the backyard, I peer up toward the kitchen window—it looks right out over the back patio—wondering where my parents are.

"Over here," Kimmie shouts, moving toward the bulkhead doors.

"Shh . . ." Wes scolds her. "You want a party out here?"

Still, I hang back for a bit, feeling my adrenaline peak, not quite ready to see the message again.

"Holy shit!" Wes shouts, standing with Kimmie right in front of the bulkhead now. "You seriously have to check this out." He scoots down to examine the metal doors with his magnifying glass. "It's even worse than you said. I mean, this isn't just scary—"

"It's scarce," Kimmie says.

Wes goes in for a closer look, his magnifying glass practically welded to his eye.

"What's wrong?" I ask, sensing their sarcasm.

But instead of answering, Wes unscrews the cap off his bottle of nail polish remover, spills some out onto a rag, and then wipes the door's surface. "Just as I expected," he says, showing Kimmie the result on the rag.

Kimmie shakes her head. "Okay, so now I really *am* worried."

"Well, she *does* claim to hear voices." He snickers.

She folds her arms, tapping the toe of her wedge-heeled boot against the frozen ground. "Diagnosis?"

"Schizophrenic," he says. "With a tendency toward hallucinations."

"What are you guys talking about?" I finally join them at the bulkhead to look.

The message is gone. Vanished. As if it was never there.

"Wait, what's going on?" I ask, as if they have the answers. As if they're the ones responsible.

"*Nothing's* going on," Wes says. "That's the problem." He flashes me the empty rag. "Not even a speck of residual color."

"It was here," I insist, grabbing at the sudden ache in my head. "You have to believe me."

"We do believe you," Kimmie says, resting a hand on my shoulder.

"But you're obviously really stressed," Wes continues.

"This has nothing to do with me being stressed. That message was there. It said 'You're Dead.'"

"What's up with a message like that, anyway?" Wes asks. "I mean, you're not dead. You're clearly alive."

"She could be a ghost." Nate laughs.

Wes tilts his head in thought, as if considering the idea.

"Make fun if you want, but I have proof." I show them

my thumb, still red from the smear of writing.

"Um . . . okay," Wes says, giving Kimmie a look like I'm full-on crazy.

"What's wrong?" I ask.

"Only that you work in a ceramics studio," he says.

"Where they have lots of paint," Kimmie continues, "and where you're bound to get said paint on your fingers."

"You don't understand," I explain. "I wet my finger in the snow. That's how I rubbed some of the writing off the bulkhead."

"Definitely not a Sharpie, then," Wes says. "That stuff doesn't wash off so easily." He douses his rag with more of the nail polish remover and wipes the entire bulkhead area. "Nothing," he says, showing us the clean rag. "I don't see anything under the magnifying lens either."

"Maybe your dad washed it," Kimmie says.

"Maybe I washed what?" Dad peeps over the fence, then unlocks the gate and grabs a couple logs of firewood.

I open my mouth, trying to think of a clever way to ask him, but then I just say it: "Were you out here earlier?"

"That depends . . . earlier as in ten minutes ago?"

"More like an hour?"

"Then, no," he says, moving closer to study my face. "Why, is there something wrong?" He looks toward the bulkhead, curious as to why we're all standing around it.

"I was just wondering if you saw us come back here."

"I didn't even know you were home." He smiles. "I thought you went for a walk. You kids want a snack? I've got a secret stash of Cheetos inside."

"No thanks," Wes says. "I should probably get going. My dad wants me to see some wrestling thing on TV with him later. Apparently watching sweaty fat men pulverize each other is what normal guys do."

"Well, if *you're* going, then we're getting a ride," Kimmie says, motioning for Nate to join them. "Camelia, call me later, okay?"

I nod and watch them leave.

"Are you coming inside?" Dad asks, once we're alone.

"In a couple minutes," I say, giving him some sorry excuse about how I'm feeling slightly sun deprived and would like to stay out for a little bit longer.

He glances once more at the bulkhead, clearly not buying my BS, but luckily he doesn't probe any deeper.

I wait until he goes back inside before continuing to check out the bulkhead. I scour the doors from different angles, still able to picture the message in my mind's eye. But, like Wes, I honestly can't find even a single speck of evidence that the writing was ever here.

35

April 9, 1984

Dear Diary,

It's getting harder and harder at school. Today Morgan McCarthy and her group of lemmings were talking about me in art class. They kept staring at me and then laughing really loud when I looked. Toward the end of class, Jamie Freeman, Morgan's on-again-off-again boyfriend, walked by and tried to sneak a peek at what I was painting.

But my canvas was blank. After what happened to my mother with her fall and stitches, I'm almost too afraid to do anything artistic. I feel like there's something very wrong with me. Everyone knows it, too. Nobody in school talks to me. I eat alone. I do labs by myself. I sit in the corner of almost every class.

The teachers don't know what to do with me. The guidance counselor doesn't either. She brought me in to her office to talk, but it was almost as if she was afraid of me too. She could barely even look at me, kept fidgeting with the crucifix around her neck, like maybe in some way I was evil and she was trying to ward me off.

I asked her if I could get out of art class, saying how the kids were giving me trouble. Instead of trying to resolve the problem, as I assumed she would have, she barely even blinked an eye before switching me into study hall for the remainder of the year.

It's like everyone around here jumps through hoops for me. I can part the sea of people just by walking down the hallway. But if I'm supposedly so important, how come nobody ever asks me how I'm feeling?

Love,
Alexia

36

*J*N MY ROOM, I grab a notebook and sit at the computer, determined to find some answers. I type the word "psychometry" into at least five different search engines, but they all end up bringing me to sites I've already seen. And so I refine my search, pairing the word "psychometry" with the words "hearing voices" in an effort to find some connection.

I end up coming across a blog entitled "Psychometrically Suzy." In it, the woman, Suzy, writes about how one day a few months ago, when she was cleaning out her hallway closet, she came across her father's old hat. She says that when she ran her fingers along the brim, she was able to hear her father's voice, even though he'd been dead for over fourteen years.

At first she thought the voice was coming from somewhere inside her house. She also wondered if maybe it was a neighbor or a passerby outside her window, and the similarity of the voice was just a mere coincidence. But somewhere deep inside her, she couldn't shake the feeling that it was her dad. That it was *his* voice, with its familiar raspy quality and the endearing way he'd called her by her full name, Suzanne, rather than Suzy, like everyone else.

Apparently, the voice kept calling out to her, leading her into the living room. It wasn't long before she realized that the voice was coming from inside her head, because aside from herself, the house was empty. And no one was outside.

As soon as she reached the living room mantel, and a photo sitting on top of it, the voice finally stopped. The photo was a snapshot of her with her dad. "It was as if he wanted me to see us together again," Suzy wrote. "And in that moment, though he had long since passed away, we *were* together again."

Suzy goes on to write about other instances involving touch—episodes where she'd get a picture in her head or a vague feeling of doom—but nothing as strong as actually hearing a voice like that day with her dad.

I sink back in my seat, wondering if maybe that's why I've had only two instances of hearing voices but yet several episodes where I've sculpted bits from my future. Maybe hearing voices only occurs when something really important is happening, like with the message on the bulkhead.

Part of me is tempted to google the word "psychometry," along with the words "seeing things" or "having visions." But I know I didn't just imagine that message. I know it was there. I touched the letters. I felt the cold, hard chill of the bulkhead doors as droplets of icy water dripped over the words. I stare down at my thumb, confident that, aside from some clay residue, my fingers were clean before I touched the writing. I haven't used glaze in well over a week, and even then it was an oatmeal color. There's no other way around it: someone must have erased the message.

I write the words "Be careful" at the top of my notebook page, wondering what the voice in my head was warning me about, and why it was followed by laughter.

A second later, the phone rings, startling me. "Hello?" I answer.

"Hey," Ben says. "I hope I'm not bothering you. Is it okay that I'm calling?"

"No," I say, completely flustered. The tip of my pencil snaps under pressure. "I mean, yes. It's okay."

"I just thought I'd check in."

"Is there something wrong?"

"No."

"Then why are you calling?" I ask, realizing how abrasive that sounds, but also knowing that it needs to be said. How else am I supposed to get over him?

"It's just that when I was cleaning my room today, I came across something of yours . . . your sweatshirt. The blue one, from the other night.

"The other night?"

"Yeah," he says, his voice barely above a whisper. "When I came to your room . . . . I think I must have thought it was mine. I dashed out of there pretty quick. I didn't want you to get in trouble."

"Right," I say, trying to breathe through the pummeling sensation inside my chest.

"I could bring it by," he says.

I'm tempted to say yes, but instead I tell him to leave it on one of the coat hooks in my homeroom. "I'll find it there, no problem."

"Okay," he says. "That's probably the easiest."

But it actually couldn't be harder.

"Are you okay?" he asks, noticing maybe how distant I sound.

"Yeah," I lie, keeping a firm grip on the phone as if it can bring me stability.

"It's just so weird, isn't it?" he says. "Seeing each other in school, but not really talking?"

I nod even though he can't see me, wanting so badly to open up, to invite him in by saying something really great, but instead I remain silent.

"So, how are things going?" he ventures, still looking to talk.

I gaze at the computer. Suzy's blog is still up on the screen. "I had one of those weird sculpture episodes again."

"You sculpted something and then saw it later?"

"Not exactly," I say, hesitant to tell him about the voice.

"Then what?"

"Maybe I should go."

"Wait, Camelia, no. Does this have anything to do

with that guy you're seeing? Adam's his name, right?"

"Why would it have something to do with him?"

"Just curious," he says. "So then, it's true. You *are* seeing him?"

"I have to go," I say, frustrated by his lame attempt to get information when he no longer has the right to ask.

"Look, I'm sorry," he says. "Just try not to overanalyze things. With your sculpture episodes, I mean. Sometimes it's best to just go with the flow. To see where impulse takes you."

"Is that the real reason you called?" I ask, wondering if he's going with his impulses too.

"I'll leave your sweatshirt in your homeroom," he says, ignoring the question.

We hang up shortly after, and my heart keeps pounding. A few moments later, the phone rings again. This time it's Kimmie.

"How are you doing?" she asks.

"You don't seriously think I'm schizo, do you?"

"Honestly?" She pauses for drama. "No. Did you talk to your dad?"

"Negative."

"Okay, you really *are* nuts. Why do you think I left in such a rush? I thought maybe you could talk to him then."

"I'm just afraid if I tell my parents that I'm hearing voices and seeing things, they'll start comparing me to Aunt Alexia."

"Calling you suicidal?"

"More like mentally unstable, which can lead to suicide attempts as evidenced by my aunt. My parents will have me brain scanned and evaluated by a shrink before you can say straitjacket."

"You can't honestly tell me that's why you're not saying anything to them."

"My mom's going through a tough time again," I explain. "Plus, I trust what Ben said. He didn't sense any danger when he touched me."

"Or so he says."

"He wouldn't lie about something that important. He called me, by the way."

"You're certainly one for withholding information. Dish, please."

"There actually isn't too much dish. He accidentally took my sweatshirt from my bedroom the other night."

"Wait, are you kidding me? Touch Boy doesn't just take *anything* by accident."

"How do you know?"

"He doesn't like to touch things, remember? I mean, Holy HOLY! Do you honestly realize how romantic that is? He took your sweatshirt . . . something you had on your body. It carried your vibe. And he kept it without saying anything for, like, one whole week."

"Maybe you're reading too much into it."

"And maybe you *should* get your head checked. That boy is scorching for you big time."

"Well, I don't know if I'd go that far."

"So, what do you think he was doing with your

sweatshirt all this time?" she asks; I can hear the wicked grin on her face. "Trying to get information about Adam, perhaps? Or just sleeping with it under his pillow, picturing you lying next to him?"

"Be serious."

"And now he's willing to give it back," she continues, "because, let's face it; he's probably pawed the thing so much that all your vibe has worn off. Not to mention that returning it gives him the perfect opportunity to see you again."

"Not quite," I say. "He's leaving it in my homeroom."

Kimmie lets out an obnoxious faux snore.

"I have to go," I say, talking over the sound.

"Right," she says. "You have a phone call to make and a sweatshirt to retrieve."

"Call me later if you need to talk."

"Yeah, you too."

We say our good-byes and hang up, but I have no intention of calling Ben back. He made his decision about where our relationship stands.

And now he has to live with it.

37

*M*Y CELL PHONE RINGS, startling me awake. I roll over to glance at the clock. It's 3:05 a.m. I roll back over, figuring it must be a wrong number, waiting for my voice mail to pick up. But then it dawns on me that it might be Kimmie—that she might be having a problem at home—and I reach for my bag to retrieve my phone.

"Hello," I whisper, folding it open. My voice is a tired slur.

No one answers.

"Kimmie?" I ask, speaking louder this time. I check the caller ID, but the number is blocked. "Either say something or I'm going to hang up."

Someone's breathing on the other end. I can hear a slight whistling sound, but the caller still remains silent.

I sit up in bed and glance toward the window. The shade and pane are both pulled down. I wait a few more seconds, just about to shut the phone, but then I hear a crinkling noise on the other end. "Hello?" I repeat.

"Be careful," the voice whispers finally.

"Who is this?" I ask, once again unable to tell if it's a male or female.

"Be careful," the voice repeats.

"Excuse me?" I ask, wondering if I'm hearing right. Those were the same words that played in my head earlier, when I was sculpting the horse statue.

"If you're not careful, you might just wind up as victim number-three."

"Who is this?" I ask again.

"You'll be dead," the voice hisses, ignoring the question. "Do I have to put it in writing? Oh, wait, I already did. I hope you got my message." A menacing giggle ripples through the phone.

A second later the phone clicks off.

Meanwhile, there's a knifelike sensation stuck beneath my ribs, making it hard to breathe. I'm tempted to turn on my night table lamp, to scream until my throat burns raw, or to go rushing into my parents' bedroom to tell them every detail.

But instead I can't seem to move. And so I burrow my head underneath the covers, hoping the darkness will hide me.

38

*A*T SCHOOL THE FOLLOWING MORNING, I head to the counselor's office, completely at a loss for what else to do. Ms. Beady seems receptive to seeing me, which helps put some of my reluctance at ease. Instead of sitting behind her giant block of a desk, she points me toward the cushy chairs in the corner of her office, and then offers me a cup of tea.

"No, thanks," I say, taking a seat, not really knowing where to begin.

"So, how are things going?" she asks. "Are you feeling a bit more secure? We spoke last time about all the pranks going on here at school."

"We spoke about me getting trapped inside the girls' bathroom," I correct her.

"Right." She purses her lips.

"I told you about the lights being shut off," I continue, "and about the note that got slipped underneath the door."

"And the note said . . . if I recall . . ." She flips back and forth in the pages of her notebook.

"It said I was next."

She looks up and nods uneasily.

"Maybe this was a mistake," I say.

"No, Camelia, stay. There's no need to get upset. I'm listening. I want to hear you."

"It hasn't stopped," I whisper.

"What hasn't?" She angles herself more toward me.

"Stuff. Like what happened in the bathroom."

"More pranks?"

"Except they're not pranks," I insist.

"Well then, why don't you tell me what they are?"

I bite my lip, wondering if she's only being patronizing—if, in her mind, she's already got this whole thing figured out. I look toward her walls, taking note of all her degrees: a bachelor's from SUNY, a master's from Yale, and a PhD from the University of Texas.

She must really know something.

"Camelia?" she asks, checking her watch.

"I heard a voice," I say.

"What kind of voice?" The expression on her face doesn't show even a hint of surprise.

"A female one. It told me to be careful."

"I see," she says, studying my face, maybe trying to judge whether or not to believe me. "And what did this voice want you to be careful *of*?"

"I don't know. That's just it; it wasn't clear at the time. But then later, I got a phone call, and the caller told me the same thing . . . to be careful."

"I see," she says, taking more notes. "So the second time you heard the voice, it was over the phone. And the first time?"

I feel my eyes begin to water.

"You can say it, Camelia. Don't be afraid to tell me whatever's going on."

"I heard it in my head," I whisper. "It was like the voice was leading me outside. And then, when I *got* outside, there was some writing scribbled on the bulkhead doors."

"Did you show it to your parents?"

I shake my head. "It was gone before I could."

Her face furrows for just a moment, before going neutral again.

"Someone must have erased it," I continue.

"Was that the first time something like that happened? The first time you saw something was there and then it wasn't? The first time you heard a voice in the way you describe . . . inside your head?"

"No," I say, feeling my lower lip tremble.

"Do you want to tell me about the other times, then?" she asks, getting me a glass of water.

I take a sip, hesitant to say anything more, but for some reason I do. I tell her about last week, when I heard Ben's voice calling out to me in the basement, and then leading me up to my bedroom.

"And no one was in your bedroom when you got there?" she asks.

"No, but I saw someone outside . . . across the street."

"Who was it?"

"I don't know. They were gone before I could tell."

"I see," she says again, a look of self-assurance on her face. "And so that person disappeared too."

"I know how all this must sound."

"You do?"

"Like I'm crazy?"

"Crazy is a word I don't like to use. But, no," she says, setting her glasses on top of her head. "I don't think you're crazy."

"Then what?" I ask, wishing there could be an easy answer.

"I think people who've been through something traumatic—something like what you went through last semester—can experience a backlash of stress. That stress can play out in a multitude of forms, from hearing voices to bouts of pure paranoia."

"Is that what you think this is? Stress?"

"Posttraumatic stress to be exact. But just to be sure, we could have you evaluated. I'd be happy to recommend someone in town. Have you spoken to your parents about all of this yet?"

I shake my head. "And you won't tell them, right?"

"I could help *you* tell them if you'd like. But, no, I'm only obligated to tell parents when I think the child is in danger. But even so, I really think your parents should know. I really think they'd *want* to know."

"I'll think about it," I say, grateful that I didn't tell her anything else, especially about what the caller said, how if I'm not careful, I'll wind up dead.

39

INSTEAD OF GOING to the cafeteria for our free
block, Kimmie and I head to the library, picking
a relatively isolated corner of the reference area. I
tell her about the phone call I got last night and how the
caller told me to be careful, just like the voice I heard in
the basement.

"The voice inside your head," Kimmie says to be clear.

"Right," I say, proceeding to tell her how the caller
also insinuated writing the message on the bulkhead.

"And did the voice inside your head tell you that too?"

"No," I say, thinking how the voice in my head
sounded altogether different—more concerned, less menacing. The giggling was different too. The laughter inside
my head sounded almost genuine, whereas the caller's was
definitely meant to intimidate.

"Well, whatever, so there's your proof." Kimmie props
an encyclopedia up beside us as coverage. "You're not

going crazy. That message was there. Someone had to have erased it."

"Except the words on the bulkhead were a little different from what the caller said; *'You're dead'* as opposed to *'you will be dead.'*"

"Close enough, especially when the caller said she put it in writing."

"She?"

"Or he. I'm only assuming it's a she, since the voice in your head was female."

"But the voice the first time was a male," I remind her. "Remember, it sounded like Ben's. . . ."

"To further complicate things . . ." She peeks out from over the top of the encyclopedia. Mr. Wayland, the librarian, is too busy showing Lily (peace-loving) Randall how to use an online database to care that we're speaking in hushed tones.

"So why do you think whoever wrote that message decided to erase it?" I ask. "I mean, why put it there only to erase it a little while after—"

"And then call to make sure you got it," Kimmie continues. "I know; it's totally messed up. But maybe the person was forced to erase it for some reason. Maybe someone saw them do it."

"Like who?"

"Who do I look like, Nancy freakin' Drew?"

"More like Madonna from the '80s," I say, referring to her fingerless lace gloves and dangling crucifix earrings.

"I'll take that as a compliment," she says, readjusting

her black leather headband. "Did you get your sweatshirt back, by the way?"

I shake my head, suddenly realizing that I didn't notice it in homeroom today.

"And so you went to Ms. Beady about it?"

"No. I went to Ms. Beady because I needed advice and I wanted perspective."

"And you thought of her? The woman wears gaucho pants and moccasins, for God's sake."

"Apparel aside, I wanted to talk to someone who's qualified. I mean, no offense. It's just that it made sense at the time to sit down with someone outside my immediate circle . . . someone with authority, who deals with people's problems on a regular basis. . . ."

"Ms. Beady is the devil," Kimmie says, using her pencil as a makeshift pitchfork to stab the table. She reminds me how last year, during the pep rally, Ms. Beady sent her home for wearing a cheerleading outfit adorned with spikes and chains. "The spikes and chains weren't even real."

"How dare she?" I mock, gazing at the window beside me, where someone's left a cheat sheet on the ledge.

"Exactly," Kimmie says. "Which is why I can't even believe you went looking for her advice. You want my advice? You need to go talk to Debbie."

"Why would I talk to *her*?"

"The caller *did* mention you'd be victim number-three. . . ."

I shake my head, still unable to follow her logic.

180

"Seriously, are the moldy encyclopedia fumes getting to you?" she asks. "Victim number-one is already dead."

"You mean Julie?"

"Do you know any other dead victims? And so, seeing as Julie's deadness makes it just a tad bit difficult to communicate, maybe victim number-two has some answers."

"Well, here's my question: why aren't *I* a victim. Was I not tied up and left in the back of a trailer four months ago?"

"That's just it." Her face softens. "Whoever this is doesn't consider you a victim."

"Because I'm not a victim of Ben's," I say, meeting her eyes.

"Time to talk to your parents now?"

I nod, knowing I have no other choice. "But first I'm going to talk to Debbie."

40

I TRACK DEBBIE MARCUS down in front of the
school as she's waiting for the late-bus to arrive.
She looks in my direction and then quickly turns
away, as though I'm the last person on the planet she wants
to see right now.

"Hey." I approach her anyway.

"What do you want?" she asks, fidgeting with the scarf
around her neck.

"I was hoping we could talk for a second."

"Not if it involves you trying to tell me what a swell
guy Ben is, or how I need to give him a chance, or how I'm
seeing things all distorted."

"It sounds like somebody's already been talking to
you."

"Whatever," she says, pulling her ski hat down over
her ears, perhaps to block me out. Only a few stray
auburn curls peek out from under the rim. "Ben is the

reason I was in a coma. End of story. Is that why you wanted to chat?"

"I'm not here to defend Ben."

"Then why *are* you here?" She turns to face me. There are giant circles under her eyes from lack of sleep, and her face appears less freckled than I remember.

"I got this weird phone call," I tell her. "The person on the other end said that if I'm not careful, I'll be victim number-three."

"And?" she asks, seemingly unsurprised.

"And you don't think that's weird?"

"I think there are a bunch of losers at this school who like to play games, as evidenced by what happened to me," she says.

"But you don't even blame them," I say. "You blame Ben. Why is that?"

"Because, if you must know, I think Ben's the one who hit me that night."

"A car hit you."

"Maybe Ben was driving it. All the witness said was that it was a dark car. Ben's aunt drives a black sedan. Ever think that maybe he arranged the whole thing? Maybe he dropped his motorcycle off at home and then took her keys."

"Your friends were the ones stalking you. Even you admit that."

"So?"

"So, Ben had no reason to come after you."

"My friends may have been playing up some of the

stalker stuff for laughs, but no one can deny the way Ben stared me down in class . . . and how he used to follow me around on occasion."

"Do you seriously believe that?" I ask, shaking my head, wondering how she can twist things around so much.

"Plus," she continues, "for all I know that so-called 'witness' standing in front of Finz at just the right time could totally have been a friend of Ben's. Tell me that isn't possible."

I sink my teeth deep into my lip, not knowing what to say, or how to answer.

"Exactly," she says, when I don't respond. "Maybe that caller's right. Maybe if you aren't careful, you *will* end up victim number-three. I wouldn't even be surprised if Ben was the one who called you."

"Ben saved my life," I remind her. *"Twice."*

She shrugs, like it doesn't matter. "He's smart. I'll give him that."

"What's that supposed to mean?"

"It's like that with all wackos. They're completely normal on the outside, but it's all a facade. They use that nice little Boy Scout exterior to their advantage, to hide the darker parts of themselves."

A second later, the late-bus pulls into the traffic circle.

"You don't know what you're talking about," I say.

"No!" she barks. *"You* don't. Ben doesn't belong here. Things were just fine before he arrived. Even you can't deny that."

"I can," I say, feeling my chin tremble. "If it wasn't for

Ben, I wouldn't even be here right now."

The doors of the bus creak open. "Do yourself a favor," she says. "Tell the principal about that phone call you got; tell your parents, and tell the police."

"Even if it's a joke, like you say?"

"Being tied up in the back of someone's trailer isn't a joke; neither is spending over two months in a coma."

"But you're doing so well now," I remind her. "I mean, don't you think there comes a point where you have to stop looking back? When you should finally move on?"

Her pale blue eyes narrow, as if she can't quite grasp my words. "My grandfather died while I was in that coma. My parents said it was too much for him."

"Debbie, I'm sorry. I had no idea."

"Sorry doesn't change it, though. It doesn't change the fact that I never got to say good-bye. . . . That he was so worried I'd never make it out of the coma that his heart couldn't handle it."

"I'm sorry," I repeat, for lack of better words, finally able to understand her need to assign blame.

"I gotta go," she says again, wiping her runny eyes with her mitten.

"Are you sure?" I ask, wishing we could talk more.

Debbie doesn't answer. Instead she climbs the school-bus steps. And the doors slam shut behind her.

41

May 6, 1984

Dear Diary,

Sometimes I wonder what my life would've been like if my father hadn't left my mother. I wonder if she would have loved me, and if I'd be wanted.

My mother left Jilly's father shortly before my dad came into the picture, so Jilly and me are only half-sisters. Jilly says she doesn't remember too much about it, but she thinks our mother must have really loved my father. And then when I came along, it ruined everything.

Alexia

42

*W*HEN I GET HOME from school, my parents are sitting at the kitchen island waiting for me.

"What's going on?" I ask, dropping my backpack to the floor. I glance at the clock. It's a little after four. "Dad, why aren't you still at work?"

"Your mother asked me to come home."

"Why?" My pulse starts to race.

Dad's brown eyes narrow. "Is there something you want to tell us about?"

"What do you mean?" I ask, wondering what they might know, if Kimmie or Ms. Beady talked to them.

"You aren't keeping things from us again, are you, sweetie?" Mom asks.

Dad runs his fingers through his thick dark hair, the sides of which are starting to gray.

"Is it Aunt Alexia?" I ask, suspecting that it isn't.

"It's *you*," Mom says. Her hands quiver as she retrieves a postal-wrapped package from her lap and slides it across the island toward me. "At least, it's addressed to you. It was delivered with today's mail."

The package is about the size of a concrete block. My name and address are scribbled across the surface, but there's no return address.

"Do you have any idea who it might be from?" she continues.

I shake my head, trying to appear calm, but my head starts spinning and I need to sit down.

"I don't think she should open it," Dad tells Mom.

"Well then, you open it for her," Mom says, getting up from the island. She pours two mugs of dandelion tea and sets one of them in front of me.

"I'll open it," I say.

"Are you sure?" Dad asks.

I hesitate but then manage a nod, noticing how the package was actually mailed. There are postal marks in the corner. I reach out to take it, surprised at how light it is. Mom offers me a pair of scissors for the taped-up seams. I cut the sides open, finally unwrapping the entire package.

It's a dark blue box.

"No card?" Mom asks, leaning closer to look.

I flip the box over in my hands, noticing the moisture in my palms. "I guess not," I whisper, wondering who it could be from.

Slowly, I remove the cover. Wads of crumpled tissue

paper collect on top. I pick through them, finally able to see the object inside.

"What is it?" Mom asks.

It appears to be a wooden box of some sort. I lift the object out, despite my dad's protests to do it for me. Popsicle sticks have been glued together to form the model of a shop. The sign on the top reads "Camelia's House of Clay."

I grab the gift tag attached and flip it over to read the message, feeling a megawatt smile illuminate my face.

"Well?" Mom asks. "What does it say?"

"'Here's to an interesting journey,'" I say, reading the words aloud.

"And who's it from?"

"Adam." I flash them the card where he's signed his name.

A huge rush of relief runs over my body as I explain to them how I told Adam I wanted to open up my own pottery shop one day. "And since he wants to be an architect . . ." I continue, marveling at the clever design. There's a pair of double doors at the front that open, revealing a studio area and what appears to be a kiln room in the back. I lift the roof to peer inside, noting the care he took in creating tables and storage shelves for pottery pieces.

"Why didn't he include a return address?" Mom asks. "Where does this boy live?"

"Jilly, relax," Dad tells her. "His name isn't Matt."

"Not funny," she snaps.

"You should go call him," Dad says to me.

"Better yet, I have to work in a bit," I say. "I think I'd rather thank him in person."

Dad grabs the keys and tells me he'll give me a ride. But instead of taking me straight to Knead, he pulls into the drive-through of Taco Bell for a quick side order of nachos and cheese. "You have a couple minutes, right?" he asks, turning into a parking spot.

I look toward the digital clock on the dashboard. "About twenty minutes before my shift starts." Just enough time to fill him in on stuff.

"Well, this won't take long," he says, using the console as a makeshift table. "We'll have these polished off in no time." He peels the lid off the cheese sauce and offers me first dibs on the chips.

"So I was relieved about the package you got today," he says, watching as I take a bite. "Adam seems like a really nice guy."

I nod, suspecting there's far more on Dad's agenda than just Adam's niceness and nachos with cheese.

"You haven't received any other packages, have you?" he asks. "Because you know you can tell me anything, right?"

"Right," I say, relieved that he's brought it up.

"And I know you haven't been sleeping the greatest lately," he continues. "At least I've heard you get up a couple times in the middle of the night to go downstairs and work on your stuff. I'm assuming that can't all be attributed to nighttime artistic inspiration. Can it?"

"I guess not," I admit.

"But you don't have anything to report?" He studies my expression, trying to tell if I'm lying.

"Well, there have been a lot of pranks going on at school," I venture. "Even with me."

"For instance?" he asks, without missing a beat.

And so I tell him about the bathroom incident and how someone hung a G.I. Jane doll in the center of the hallway. "They tied the doll in place with a jump-rope-turned noose. And then a bunch of kids were batting it back and forth like a lame-o game of handball."

"Did the principal or anyone do anything about it?"

I shrug, vaguely remembering hearing something about how a couple of the boys got detention, but the administration couldn't really do anything serious since no one would fess up to hanging the doll in the first place. "There's supposed to be an assembly coming up. Ms. Beady said something about the school instituting a no-tolerance policy for pranks."

"Well, it'd better be sooner rather than later, because obviously some jokes can get out of hand."

I nod, thinking about Debbie and how she had said something similar.

Dad and I sit in silence for a few more minutes, just the sound of each other's crunching as we finish off the remainder of chips and dip. In my mind, I try to formulate the words to tell him everything. The thing is, it all sounds so crazy inside my head. I can only imagine how it'll sound to him.

I look toward the side of his face, confident that, crazy

or not, he still deserves to know the truth, that it wasn't fair of me to keep things from him and Mom last semester, and that part of the reason I ended up in trouble was because of those secrets.

"Dad," I begin, my voice barely above a whisper.

"I'm really glad we had this chat," he says, obviously not having heard me. "Sometimes I think things get a little hectic at home and we forget to take a pause."

"Now you sound like Mom."

"Which brings me to the next item on my agenda. If things between your mom and me seem a little intense lately, know that it has nothing to do with you."

"Intense?" I ask, feeling the surprise on my face.

"I think therapy has been good for your mom, but it's also brought out some unresolved issues from her childhood. Issues that I wasn't there for and can't understand completely . . . or at least not in the way that she wants me to. Add that to the stress she still feels about you—"

"Why *me?*"

"About what happened this past fall," he clarifies.

"Oh," I say, biting down on my tongue.

"Bottom line," he continues, "your mom is going through some pretty tough stuff right now. And I love her more than anything. I just need to remind myself to have patience, you know?"

"Yeah," I say, not fully sure what I'm agreeing to. "Are you guys okay?"

"We'll be just fine." He gives a less-than-reassuring pat to my lap. "Now, what do you say we get you to work?"

I manage a nod, and Dad puts the car in reverse, backing out of the parking spot. We pull up in front of Knead not three minutes later. He gives me a quick peck on the cheek and pulls away. Meanwhile, inside my head is a tangle of confusion.

Spencer notices. "Are you okay?" he mouths almost as soon as I come through the door. He's teaching a group of moms how to paint using a crackle glaze.

I give him the thumbs-up and then move toward the stairwell, taking a moment at the very top. It just seems so surreal. I mean, all along I thought I was the one keeping secrets from my parents, but it seems they've been keeping them from me too.

A few breaths later, I move down the stairs, eager for a diversion. Adam has his back to me. He removes several thick rubber bands from a huge block of a mold, and then, using all his strength—I can see the veins in his forearms pop—separates both mold halves.

"The elephant table," I say, recognizing the piece. The very top of the elephant's back has a flat surface, enabling someone to affix a piece of glass, creating a tacky table.

"I've been pulling these since two," he says, gesturing to the stampede of elephants collected in the corner.

"So, I got your gift in the mail today," I say. "Thank you. It was really cute and really thoughtful."

"Yeah well, that's me," he jokes, wiping his clay-covered fingers on a rag. He moves closer, a beaming smile stretched across his face. "You inspired me the other night. I had a great time."

"Really?"

"Is that so hard to believe?" He reaches out to touch my hands. The residual clay on his fingers feels gritty against my skin. "So, what do you say we do it again?" he asks. "Are you free after work? We could try out the new pizza place across the street."

"Regino's?"

Adam inches even closer, sliding his fingers in between mine. "Yeah, I think that's what it's called."

"Except it isn't new."

"It's all new to me." He smiles. There's a smear of clay slip on his cheek. "I've only been here a couple weeks, remember?"

"Right."

"So, is that a yes to the pizza?"

At the same moment, a piece of greenware catches my eye and I have to pull away. It's a ceramic tree. Its limbs branch out in sharp angles, twisting together, and reminding me of Ben. Of the scar on his arm.

"Is everything okay?" Adam asks.

"Yeah," I lie.

"Hey, if pizza's not your thing, we could always do Chinese."

"No," I say. "Pizza's fine. I should probably just get upstairs." The image of Ben's scar still vivid in my mind, I move quickly up the steps, anxious to get to work.

43

*A*FTER WORK I CALL my parents to tell them I'm all set with a ride home, then Adam and I head over to Regino's for a large cheese pizza with mushrooms. We sit at a table toward the back, the top of which is covered with a sticky vinyl tablecloth.

"Are you sure everything's okay?" Adam asks. "Because you seemed a little out of it at work."

"I guess I have a lot on my mind." I gaze out the window beside us, where a tall barren tree branches out in our direction, all but touching the glass pane.

"That seems to be the norm with you," he says.

"Well, I don't know if it's normal, but it's definitely me."

"Does it have something to do with that guy you were seeing? The one who went away but then came back . . . the one you were waiting for?"

"Not exactly," I say, looking back at him.

"What's the deal with him, anyway?" He takes a sip

from his root beer mug. "You guys still have something going?"

"Not exactly," I repeat.

His eyebrows go up, as if in surprise. "You don't sound so sure."

"Ben and I are just friends." Barely friends, actually.

"But you want it to be more?"

I look over my shoulder, suddenly feeling warm.

"I mean, I don't want to get all up-close-and-personal in your business or anything," he continues. "It's just that I like you. And I'd kind of like to be clear on things before I get too attached."

"Really?" I grin.

"Are you a heartbreaker?" He winks to be funny.

"Hardly."

"Then what's the deal?"

"The deal is that, yes, there's some personal stuff going on with me right now. But no, Ben is no longer my boyfriend." I don't know that he ever was.

"So why did you guys break up, then?"

"Are you sure you want to talk about this?"

"It's the third date, if you count the coffee shop; aren't we *supposed* to talk about this stuff now?"

I shift uneasily, almost forgetting that this *is* a date, and that things are obviously starting to progress. "I didn't know there was a handbook on when-to-talk-about-what when you're dating," I say to redeem myself.

"Are you kidding?" His brown eyes crinkle in a smile. "I wrote the book."

"Well, in that case . . ."

And so I give him some vague details about Ben, including how he was homeschooled for a while, how the first time I saw him was when he saved my life, and how he hasn't exactly been welcome at my school.

"I don't get it," he says. "How can somebody who saved your life not be the most popular guy in school?"

"Ben has a past."

"Don't we all?"

"Yeah, but his is . . . difficult. He sort of has a bad reputation."

"Sort of?" Adam asks.

I grab my root beer mug and press it against my lips. "Maybe this is a conversation for another time."

"Come on, now you've *got* to tell me," Adam insists. "I mean, how bad can it be? The guy didn't kill anyone, did he?"

My mouth drops at the irony of the remark, and I nearly choke mid-sip. Root beer burns in my throat.

"Are you okay?" Adam asks, pushing a glass of water toward me.

I nod and take a sip, trying to stifle a cough. Meanwhile, the waitress comes to deliver our pizza. "Can I get you anything else?" she asks.

I shake my head, anxious for her to leave.

Once she does, Adam takes my plate and serves me a slice. "Don't worry about all that ex info," he says. "I'll weasel it out of you eventually."

"I don't feel right talking about Ben's private life," I say, my throat finally clear.

"It must be pretty bad if even saving your life doesn't make him a hero."

"It's just that Ben has a lot of secrets."

"Okay, well now you're just being cruel."

"Actually, I think maybe I've already said too much."

"Well, let's see," he says, putting it all together. "The guy has a dark and secretive past, a bad reputation, and not many friends. I can definitely see the appeal."

"You really just have to get to know him."

"And when will that be? I'd love to meet this guy."

"Maybe in another lifetime." I take a bite of pizza, reluctant to say any more.

"Well, there's one thing I already know for sure," Adam continues. "Ben's definitely an idiot for not wanting you back; but you're probably better off."

"You think?"

"I know," he says, reaching out to touch my forearm. "And I'm better off too, because now I'm the one who gets to have pizza with you." He smiles slightly, like he really means it—like he really cares about what's happening between us.

"So, maybe we should talk about *your* ex-girlfriends now," I say.

"I have a better idea." He leans forward over the table as if he wants to kiss me, and part of me hopes he will. But then there's another part that still feels conflicted, like maybe this is all happening way too soon.

Adam stares at me hard, making my heart beat fast. I'm just about to look away, when I feel his mouth brush against my lips in a tiny kiss.

"I'm so glad I bumped into Spencer that day," he says, once the kiss breaks. "I may never have met you otherwise."

"Yeah," I say, almost tempted to kiss him back. "Me too." I gaze out the window again, suddenly wishing I'd met him at some other, less complicated time.

A moment later, a limb snaps off the tree outside, and I flinch. The branch falls to the ground with a penetrating crack that cuts right through my core.

"Is everything okay?" Adam asks.

"I'm fine," I tell him, unable to take my eyes off that tree. It looks so broken now, as if something's definitely missing.

44

*A*DAM IS GLOWING as he drives me home.
There's a huge grin on his face, and every few
seconds he turns to look at me.

I nervously tug at my ponytail, only wishing I felt the
same. It's not that I don't like him—right down to his
quirky sense of humor and how thoughtful he is with
me—it's just that my heart really isn't into this right now.
But maybe in time it will be.

I look at his profile, wanting to tell him that, but
before I can, he asks when he can see me again.

"I don't know." I shrug. "When's your next shift at
Knead?"

"Thursday," he says, pulling up in front of my house.
He puts the car in park and inches closer. "But please don't
make me wait until then."

A smile wriggles across my lips.

"Wait, did that just sound totally lame?" he asks.

I shake my head, flattered by his affection, but also knowing that if I want to pursue something real with him, I need to put Ben behind me. For good.

"Can I pick you up from school on Wednesday?" he asks.

I nod and he leans in even closer. "Good night," I say, turning my head. I feel his kiss land against my cheek.

"Good night," he whispers. There's a disappointed look on his face.

"I just need to take things slow."

"I get it," he says, perhaps slightly reassured. He manages a smile and gives my hand a tiny squeeze.

"But I'll see you Wednesday," I continue. I close the car door behind me, then linger on the sidewalk while he pulls away and takes a turn at the end of my street.

I'm just about to go inside, when I spot a moving shadow near the driveway. "Hello?" I call out, pausing just a couple yards from the front door. I look toward the motion-detector light, trying to reassure myself. If someone was there, it'd definitely go on.

But no one answers and I don't hear anything.

I move a couple steps closer to the door. At the same moment, the shadow moves from behind my mom's car. I can see it clearly now, a narrow strip of darkness that grows wider with each step, until he's only a couple feet away.

Ben.

"What are you doing here?" I ask.

Dressed in layers of charcoal and navy, his hair is

tousled and windblown and his dark gray eyes are urgent and needy.

"I was just riding around." He motions to his bike parked across the street several houses down. "And I wanted to see you. I thought I'd return that sweatshirt of yours."

"You were supposed to leave it for me at school."

"Oh, right," he says, as if just remembering. "I did leave it there. I don't know what I'm thinking."

I shake my head, completely confused, especially since I didn't see my sweatshirt in homeroom this morning.

"So, I just kind of wanted to check on you," he says, suddenly abandoning his excuse.

"What for?" I look over my shoulder at the outside light by the door, knowing that my parents are probably waiting up for me.

"Were you out with that guy again?"

"Do you honestly believe that you have any right to ask me that?"

"He didn't even walk you to the door," Ben says, coming closer. His pale smooth skin is like a slice of moonlight.

"He doesn't exactly skulk around my house either."

Ben's eyes lock on mine. "I'm not skulking," he says.

"Then what do you call it?" I ask. "Hanging around my house at night, where no one can see you?"

"You've got it all wrong," he says.

"Then why didn't you ring the doorbell?"

He gestures to my bedroom window, where the shade's drawn. "I knew you weren't home. The light's been out all night."

"You should go," I say, wondering how long he's been out here waiting for me.

"Is that really what you want?" He steps even closer, so that our faces are only inches apart. I can smell the motorcycle fumes on his clothes.

"You have no right to come here," I snap. "You have no right to sneak up on me, or ask me about other guys."

"That doesn't answer my question. Just say you want me to leave, and I'll go."

"I want you to leave," I say, hearing the quiver in my voice.

Still he doesn't move. Instead he touches me. His thigh grazes my leg as if by accident. I close my eyes, feeling an electric current pulse through my veins.

"Are you sure you want me to go?" he whispers into my ear.

"Yes," I lie, almost tempted to touch his shoulder, to rest my head against his chest, and then to kiss him until my lips ache.

His thigh still pressed against my leg—our only point of physical contact—I want more than anything to draw him even closer, to feel the heat of his body pressed against mine. *Kiss me*, I scream inside my head. His mouth is just millimeters from brushing against my cheek. I can feel his breath, a slow and rhythmic pant.

"I just wanted to check on you," he says again.

Despite the chill in the air, I can feel perspiration beading up at the back of my neck. I'm half-tempted to tear off my coat, to snake my arms underneath his jacket, and feel his pulse on my skin.

I open my eyes finally, while his remain closed. "Why did you want to check on me?" I ask. "Is there something wrong?"

He doesn't answer.

"Ben?"

"I've missed you so much," he says. At least I think that's what he said. His voice is barely above a whisper.

Part of me wants to say that I miss him too, but instead I tell him that I should go in. "My parents will be wondering where I am." I take a reluctant step back, just leaving him there.

"Good night," he says, looking back at his bike so I can't see his disappointment.

"Are you sure there's nothing else you want to tell me?" I ask.

He shakes his head and moves toward the street until I can no longer see him. There's just a shadow against the pavement now.

And an aching deep inside me.

45

ONCE INSIDE THE HOUSE, I press my back up against the door and remind myself to breathe.

"That must have been *some* date," Mom says, noticing the flushing of my cheeks, or how I can barely stand straight. "Well?" she asks.

"Good," I say, suddenly realizing that the answer doesn't even fit.

"You really like this boy, don't you?" she asks.

"I'd take that as a yes," Dad says, studying my expression.

"So, tell us about him," she insists.

I nod, trying to gain full composure, to stop the well of tears I feel filling up behind my eyes. "He's nice," I say, reluctant to tell them about Ben.

"*How* nice?" Mom asks.

I take a seat opposite them on the sofa, fully aware that my legs are still shaking. I glance toward the living room window, wondering if Ben's still outside. I haven't heard his motorcycle start up yet.

"Camelia?" Mom pushes.

"He listens when I talk," I say finally. "He seems genuinely interested in what I do. He's respectful during our time together—"

"Well, he sounds pretty perfect," Dad says.

"Are you sure that *you* don't want to date him?" Mom asks him.

"That depends. Is he a vegan, vegetarian, raw foodist, fruititarian, macro-bi-whatever, or a combination of any of the above?"

"I don't believe so," I say, eager to get away.

"Well then, I just might be tempted," he jokes.

But Mom seems in a far less joking mood. "I have to go out of town for a couple days," she says, pulling the plug on any possibility of humor. "I've decided to go meet with Aunt Alexia and her doctor. They're in Detroit."

"And just when were you planning on telling me this?" Dad asks.

"I told you before, and now I'm telling you again."

"You didn't tell me they were in Detroit."

"Well, they are," she says, defensive. She moves to the window, her back turned toward him. "And they want me to come as soon as possible."

"And when's that?" he asks. "I'll need to ask for the time off from work."

"You don't have to come with me."

"I *want* to come with you." He crosses the room and forces her to face him.

It takes some prodding, but after a few moments, she wilts into his embrace, making my heart tighten and my eyes well with tears.

Still, I have to wonder, if they go to Detroit together, who will stay with me?

I turn away and head down to my studio. My horse-in-progress is sitting on the worktable. I remove the plastic covering and close my eyes. The image of the horse resurfaces in my mind's eye like a model of sorts. I peel off my coat and get to work, somehow still able to feel the heat of Ben's thigh pressed against my leg.

I breathe through the sensation, trying to keep focused on my sculpture. I work diligently on the horse's front legs in their kicked-up position. Then I run my sponge over the horse's back, admiring the silvery clay color and the smooth texture of the horse's coat.

Several hours later, even after my dad comes down and tells me to get to bed, I remain glued to my worktable. My fingers turn waterlogged as I create the curves of the body and the muscles in the hind legs. The horse's tail whips out, as if entangled in the wind. Meanwhile, its eyes are wild, like he wants to run free.

Once finished, I take a step back to inspect my work. About fourteen inches high, the horse is exactly as I pictured, exactly as it should be.

I close my eyes, still able to see the horse's image inside my head. And still able to hear Ben's voice from tonight. When he told me how much he misses me.

46

May 25, 1984

Dear Diary,

  I haven't done art in a couple months.
And my life has never been emptier.
I thought it would've made things easier,
but instead I feel even more alone than
ever.

Alexia

47

THE FOLLOWING DAY at lunch, Kimmie, Wes, and I try our best to digest the swill du jour—something the cooks have curiously dubbed Mexican Extravaganza—made with red beans, rice pilaf, and what appears to be chunks of albacore tuna.

"Heinous," Wes says, throwing his fork down.

"Seriously, is this horse meat?" Kimmie inspects a suspicious tan glob on her fork.

"Speaking of horses," I begin, "I've decided to give my latest sculpture to Ben."

"No way," she squawks. "Adam is the one who made you that stick-figure pottery studio thingamajig. Now it's time for *you* to reciprocate with something crafty."

"Though, personally I'd have sculpted something sexier," Wes adds.

"Like what, a banana?" she asks, referring to the enthusiasm with which Wes is eating his. He practically engulfs the phallic fruit in two bites flat.

"As long as it comes with a peel," he jokes. "It's always best to play it safe."

"I'm giving Ben the sculpture because he's the one who helped inspire the piece," I explain.

"Because he reminds you of a horse?" Kimmie asks, almost spitting out a mouthful of milk.

"Impressive," Wes says, shifting uneasily in his seat.

"Because I was almost afraid to finish the piece," I correct them, "but he encouraged me to go with my impulse. To not overanalyze things."

"I like the horse analogy better."

"I saw him last night, by the way. He was at my house when Adam dropped me off."

"And?" She perks.

"And it's time we ended things."

"Again?" Wes raises an eyebrow in curiosity.

"What he means to say is, haven't you guys ended things, like, thirty times at least?" Kimmie asks.

"But this time I mean it."

"As opposed to the other twenty-nine times." She rolls her eyes, the lids highlighted by a dark purple color that reminds me of prunes.

"Adam said he wants to meet him," I venture, eager for their opinion.

"Him, as in Ben?" Kimmie asks.

"The one and only."

"Well, you can't exactly blame the guy," Wes says. "I suppose I'd want to size up the competition too."

"I'm not even sure he was serious," I say. "I mean, the idea of it is just too weird."

"No," Wes argues. "What's weird is that a guy who supposedly wants nothing more to do with you—who won't even shake your hand or talk to you in the hallway at school—keeps calling you and showing up at your house."

"Not to mention trying to come up with bogus reasons to see you," Kimmie adds, referring to my sweatshirt, which I've yet to see in homeroom, even though Ben claims to have left it there.

"Ben said he came by because he wanted to check up on me," I explain.

"What for?" Kimmie asks.

I shake my head, wishing I had an answer.

"Well, it could be either one of two possibilities," she continues. "He either A) sensed something shady when he touched you the last time, or B) still has the hots for you and wants to 'check on' how things are going between you and Adam."

"Yes, but if it's option A, then why wouldn't he tell me?"

"That's why my vote's on B," she says.

"Why don't you simply ask him?" Wes asks, gesturing to the juice machine.

Ben is standing there. He grabs his juice can from the dispenser and then pauses a moment to stare back at me.

"I thought Touch Boy avoided the cafeteria at lunch," Kimmie says.

"He does," I whisper, feeling a pummeling sensation inside my gut. "At least, he used to."

"He looks *fine*," Kimmie says, drawing the adjective out for three full syllables. She lowers her cat's-eye-shaped glasses to glare at him over the rims.

Ben continues to stare at me, making my palms sweat and my pulse quicken.

"He must be checking up on you again," she says with a wink.

"Could be," Wes agrees. "It could be sort of like what happened with me and Wendy. Even after I called it quits with her, I still wanted to know what she was up to."

"Are you seriously kidding me?" Kimmie's face goes deadpan. "You broke things off with Wendy because you were too cheap to continue paying her."

"But I still wonder how she's doing."

"Yes, but the difference is you don't continue to call her, to show up at her house, or to peep through her windows . . . or do you?"

"Negative." He lets out an exhaustive sigh. "I'm so boring and predictable."

"No, what you are is stylistically challenged." She zeros in on his sweater. "I mean, seriously, is that a Chia Pet on your chest?"

"It's called mohair."

"Are you sure you didn't simply add water and sit out in the sun?"

"Like you can talk." He gestures to her black-and-white-striped jumper with tights to match. "What do you call that . . . 'Inspired by Zebras'?"

"More like prison inmates." She rolls up a sleeve to reveal a barbed-wire tattoo. "It's fake. At least for now." The tattoo snakes up her arm and twists around her neck. "I thought I'd take advantage of my hickey by making myself look *really* trashy. I call the look 'schoolgirl gone bad.'"

"Why don't you just call it 'Kimmie'?" he asks.

While they continue to bicker, I try my hardest not to keep eyeballing Ben. He's taken a seat at a table in the corner.

"Fear not," Kimmie says, snapping me to attention. "Ben is so obviously on the brink of coming around. I wouldn't be surprised if he asks you back by the end of the week."

"It's over," I remind her. "Which is why I'm giving him my horse sculpture. It's sort of my good-bye gift."

"No offense," Wes says, trying to swallow down a chunk of tuna, "but a pound of chocolates might be a better idea."

48

*A*FTER SCHOOL, Mom asks if I want to make brownies with her. "We haven't made anything together in over a week," she says.

"Sure," I say, suddenly suspicious, especially since she's suggesting that we actually use the stove. I pull up a stool and load the food processor with the ingredients she's set out. Meanwhile, Mom melts the vegan chocolate using a double boiler.

She prattles on about our plans for the summer and how she'd like us to tour some of the colleges I'm interested in—and then she finally gets to the point: "Your father and I are leaving to visit Aunt Alexia," she says, looking up from the stove. "At least, if you're okay with it, we are."

"When?"

"Tomorrow morning, first thing. I know it's quick, but it'll only be for a couple days. It's just that the timing seems to work best for us. Aunt Alexia's therapist thinks the sooner we get there, the better."

"Because she might try something again?" I ask.

"Because she's willing to talk now. She's starting to open up about family stuff—stuff from our childhood—and she wants me there to discuss some of those things."

"You still feel guilty about her, don't you?"

She touches the monogrammed "Jilly" necklace around her neck—the one that Aunt Alexia gave her. "I just wish I'd done more to defend her, growing up. Your grandmother wasn't exactly kind to Alexia. And I didn't do much to make things better."

"I'm sure you did more than you think."

"Well, I know I did one thing." She smiles. "Did I ever tell you the reason I became a vegan?"

"Becaue of Aunt Alexia?"

"It's true. I thought it would be a surefire way to get your grandmother's anger focused on me, by being super picky about what I ate."

"And now Dad and I have to pay the consequences."

She laughs. "Who could go back to eating animal products after all that? In some weird way I thought that eating 'normally' again would be like turning my back on Alexia. I know it sounds ridiculous." Her face blushes. "After a while, the diet just stuck."

"Lucky us."

"You bet it is." She licks her finger of wannabe-chocolate. "Anyway, this trip is important. It's as if Alexia finally wants to get to the root of some of her problems."

"That's great," I say, trying to be positive.

"It really is. For a little while there, I thought things were just getting worse. She was talking about feeling alone and hearing voices."

"Hearing voices?" I ask, nearly dropping my spoon.

She nods. "I think I mentioned to you before that I didn't think she was doing so great. She kept talking so much about having voices stuck inside her head."

"What kind of voices?"

"Even she doesn't know exactly. She says they're from the future, though we're not really sure what that means."

"What does her therapist think it means?"

"I don't think she understands what's happening, from what I can tell. But she hasn't been diagnosed with schizophrenia. . . ."

"So, what *has* she been diagnosed with?"

"Nothing yet. But for now, just agreeing to meet like this is a real step in the right direction. Do you want a taste, honey?" She dips a wooden spoon into the chocolate.

I shake my head, having completely lost my appetite.

"Well, if you change your mind about us going away, I can still back out," she continues. "It's just that if I don't go now, she might not be so willing to discuss this stuff later. It's one of those strike-while-the-iron's-hot kind of things."

I gaze down at the plethora of ingredients just waiting to get processed, still trying to process everything myself. Aunt Alexia and I might have more in common than I ever thought possible.

"Is she still doing her art?" I venture.

216

"Last I heard. She's always been into watercolors and acrylics, but she's started finger painting too. At first I thought it sounded kind of childish, but I guess it helps her feel more connected to her work."

I feign a half-smile, suddenly feeling sick.

"Anyway, the timing of this trip really works for Dad's schedule," she segues. "His boss is giving him a few days off because next week he has clients coming in from out of town. He'll pretty much be working around the clock."

"And so I'm going to stay by myself?"

"I was actually hoping you wouldn't mind staying with Kimmie's family. I already called her mom and she said it was okay. That is, if you don't mind."

"I guess it's all taken care of then," I say, kind of wishing I'd been involved in at least part of the planning.

"Not if you don't want us to go."

"No," I say. "I do. It's important."

It's important that she learn more about Aunt Alexia. And it's important that Dad be there to pick up the proverbial pieces when she does.

49

*A*FTER MOM AND I finish making the brownies, I head down to my pottery studio in the basement. The horse sculpture has dried into a dark charcoal color, reminding me of some of the iron sculptures Spencer's got on display at Knead.

The detail is what strikes me most. The horse's head is cocked to one side. Its nostrils flare out and there's definite tension in the jaw. I take a step back, knowing that it's like nothing I've ever done before, which almost makes me want to show Spencer first. But instead I wrap it up in tissue paper, noting its ample weight and the way it feels beneath my fingertips, a smooth and chalky texture. I slide it into a gift bag and head up to my room.

My cell phone is ringing when I get there.

"Hey, roomie," Kimmie says when I answer. "I assume your mom told you the plan? Just don't forget to pack a bulletproof vest. It's been vicious between my parents."

"Maybe they'll play nice with company over."

"Except you're hardly company."

"What am I, then?"

"Smarter than I am in algebra. Care to help me study tonight? I have a massive test tomorrow and my head is spinning from an overdose of letters. Too many X's and Y's for my liking . . . and don't even get me started on the P's, Q's, L's, and M's."

"Well, unfortunately I have an errand to run," I say, gazing over at the gift bag.

"Can I come?"

"You have to study, remember?"

"Right," she says with a giant sigh. "Call me later?"

"You bet." After we hang up I make my way to the kitchen. Mom's just about to take the brownies out of the oven. "Care to try one while they're still hot?" she asks.

"I was actually hoping I could borrow your keys. I forgot it was Wes's birthday today," I lie. "And I'd like to drop this off for him."

"What did you get him?" She glances at the bag.

"Just something I sculpted from self-hardening clay."

"Can I see it?" She wipes her hands clean on a dish towel, preparing to take the bag.

"It's all wrapped up," I say, feeling the blood rush into my face. I keep a tight grip on the bag handles and nod toward the tissue paper.

"Oh," she says, clearly disappointed. Still, she gives me

the car keys and tells me not to be long. "Dinner's in an hour."

I turn on my heel and head out the door. Ten short minutes later, I find myself parked outside Ben's house.

I know he's home. His motorcycle's in the driveway. And so is his aunt's car—a black Pontiac sedan, just like Debbie Marcus said.

I step out of the car, confident that it wasn't Ben who hit Debbie that day. But I glance toward the front fender of his aunt's sedan anyway.

There's a dent there—a long and narrow gash that stretches around to the side, just beyond the headlight.

My hands shake, nearly dropping the gift bag. I look toward the house. The door's closed. The shades are drawn. And so I scoot down closer to inspect the dent.

There's a smear of dark red on the bumper. At the same moment, the headlights go on, shining right in my eyes. The engine roars.

I jump back, away from the tire. And then I hear the car door slam, followed by someone approaching.

"Can I help you?" a woman asks, glaring down at me. Dressed in a long wool coat and high-heeled boots, she's as tall as she is intimidating.

"Mrs. Carter?" I ask, assuming it's Ben's aunt.

"*Ms.* Carter," she says. Her mouth is a straight tense line.

I stand and extend my hand. "My name's Camelia. I'm a friend of Ben's."

"I know who you are," she says, ignoring my hand.

"Now, can I ask why you were inspecting my car?"

"I was just looking for Ben," I say, knowing the answer sounds ridiculous.

She glances toward his motorcycle—possibly checking that he's home—and swipes a few strands of her choppy dark hair away from her eyes. "Did you try ringing the doorbell?"

I shake my head, wondering what she was doing in her car, why she started her ignition and then shined her lights in my eyes. Was it to scare me?

"Do you know something about that?" she asks, gesturing to the dent in her car.

I shake my head, feeling my face flash hot.

She looks me over for several seconds, as if deciding whether or not to believe me. "Follow me," she says finally, then leads me up the front stairs.

The inside of Ben's house smells like fresh flowers and newly cut wood. I glance around, noticing potted plants lined up on all the window ledges. There's a working water fountain on the table in the living room, and the furniture is a mixture of iron and wicker.

"I'm a florist," she says, following my gaze. She takes off her coat, revealing a pair of faded jeans and a soil-stained sweatshirt.

Keeping a firm grasp on the gift bag, I glance toward the stairs. Ben's aunt watches me for a couple more seconds before calling Ben down.

No response.

She shouts his name again, louder this time, then

mutters something about how he sometimes has his head-phones on. "He can't hear a thing with those on," she says, heading up the stairs. She returns a few seconds later. "I don't know where he is." She looks out the window.

His bike is still there.

"Could I leave him something?" I ask, setting the gift bag down.

"What are you doing here?" Ben calls out from behind me. I turn to see him standing in the living room doorway.

I look toward his aunt, hoping she'll leave us alone. "I'll just be in the other room," she says, giving me one last glare.

"Don't mind her," Ben says, once she's out of earshot. "She's just being protective of me. After everything that happened last fall, it was pretty much one prank after another around here."

I nod, unsurprised.

"So, it's good to see you." He smiles, just like old times, as if there's barely been a rift between us.

"I saw you in school," I say, like it wasn't completely obvious.

"I know." His smile widens and he takes a step closer. I can smell cologne on his skin, a sweet and spicy scent.

I look up into his eyes, reminding myself to be strong. Ben's lips part, as if he wants to tell me something, but before he can, I hand him the gift. "I made you something. You don't have to open it now. Actually, I'd prefer it if you didn't."

Ben's eyebrows furrow, like he doesn't quite get it.

"It's my good-bye gift to you," I explain.

"But I'm not going anywhere."

"I know." I take a step back. "It's just . . . this is all just a little too hard for me. Being friends, and then hardly ever talking—"

"And then what happened last night?" he asks.

I nod again, feeling my whole body tremble. "I think pretending you don't exist would be easier for me than what we've been doing."

"I'm sorry," he says. "I don't want to make things more confusing for you."

I'm tempted to ask why he continues to keep tabs on me. Why he pushes me away and then comes back for more.

"This isn't easy for me either," he says.

"What do you mean?" I ask, almost wishing he'd tell me once again how much he misses me.

"Were you talking to the school counselor, by any chance?" he asks.

"Why? Did she say something to you?"

"Not just her, the principal too. They talked to me separately—first Ms. Beady, then Principal Snell. Beady pretended to be interested in my transition back to school, but then she started asking me where I'd been at certain times, whether I was hanging around the girls' bathroom on the first day of school. Sound familiar? She also wanted to know what I've been doing in my free time."

"I'm sorry," I say, though a part of me is reassured. At least the school is taking some of what I've told them seriously.

"Beady started getting all psychobabbly on me, asking if I've been upset about all the pranks going on, and how I handle my anger, whether I ever think about hurting anyone or myself. Principal Snell was less sneaky about things. He just stood there, arms folded, reminding me about the school's no-tolerance policy on pranks and hazing, and that he has no problem expelling anyone who tests it."

"Well, obviously that isn't true," I say, thinking about the G.I. Jane doll stunt in the hallway.

Ben shrugs. "There's going to be an assembly about it tomorrow."

"I can hardly wait."

Ben manages a smile and then looks down at the gift bag. "So what's this gift *really* about?"

"Like I said, part of it's a good-bye—"

"And the other part?" He stares straight into my eyes, making my stomach flip-flop.

"You told me before that I should just go with my impulses," I say, trying to stay focused. "With my pottery, I mean. You said that I shouldn't try to overanalyze things, that I should just see where my impulses take me."

"I remember."

"So, I wanted to thank you for that. This is probably my best piece yet."

"I'm glad." He smiles a bit wider. "But then maybe you should keep it."

"No," I say. "I want you to have it. If it weren't for your advice, I probably never would've finished it."

Despite what I said about not wanting him to open it now, Ben moves the tissue paper to have a peek inside.

"I have to go," I say, suddenly eager to get away. Without another look in his direction, I hurry out the door and to my mom's SUV. But then I come to a sudden halt at the sight of the windshield.

An envelope is sticking out from the wiper. With shaking hands, I pull it free and unfold it. It's a snapshot of Julie's gravestone. But someone has crossed out her name and written mine in its place.

50

June 12, 1984

Dear Diary,

Yesterday in math class, Mrs. Higley caught me scraping the paint off my desk using one of those pointy compass things. She asked me to stay after class, shook her head at the scratches I'd made, and then asked me if there was anything I wanted to talk about.

I didn't know what to say, and so I didn't really answer her. It's just that nobody's asked me that kind of stuff before.

When I got home from school, my mother told me that Mrs. Higley had called. At first I thought my mother was going to give me hell about the desk, but she didn't even mention it, so maybe Mrs. Higley didn't mention it either. According to my mother, Mrs. Higley is concerned about me. She said that I'm withdrawn and she wishes she'd said something earlier in the year.

My mother told her it's because my father left, because we're all dealing with his absence. "It's the truth, after all," my mother said. Apparently, Mrs. Higley understood completely, relieved to know my mother was so sensitive to the situation.

If only she knew the real truth.

Alexia

51

$\mathcal{W}$HEN I GET HOME from Ben's, my parents are so busy packing for their trip that we don't have dinner together; we don't even talk much.

Mom is beyond crazed. Her bed is sprinkled with at least ten different outfits. "I feel like I'm back in high school," she says, obviously clueless about what to pack. "I've left you some tuNO salad in the fridge, by the way. You can make a sandwich."

I nod and go into my room, foregoing her less-than-tempting offer for a glorified shredded parsnip sandwich, and close the door behind me. I glance toward the heap of freshly folded clothes piled high on top of my dresser, knowing that I should probably get packing too, but instead I dial Kimmie's number.

She picks up right away. "Care to explain what a polynomial is?"

"An equation with constants and variables."

"Seriously, how do you know that?"

"I gave it to him," I say, ignoring the question. "The sculpture, I mean."

"And?"

"And then I left. I didn't wait around for him to open it."

"So I guess it's over, then."

"I guess."

"Hardly," she bellows. "Steam like yours and Ben's doesn't go away after one measly kiss-off. Case in point: How many times has Ben given *you* the kiss-off? And you're still up to your eyeballs in steam."

"It's different now," I say. "At least it feels different. More final, less promising . . . so much more painful."

"Do you want me to come over?"

I shake my head as if she can hear it. "I got another photo, by the way."

"What? Where?"

And so I tell her about what happened after I fled Ben's house. "I'm almost not surprised," I say. "I mean, he said his house gets slammed with pranks."

"Right, but this prank was directed at you, not him. Plus, it follows the same pattern as the other photos."

"Actually, the writing on this photo was black, not red."

"That's not what I meant, but since you bring it up, did the writing look similar to the other notes?"

"I guess," I say, thinking how the notes were all written with capital lettering, as though in the same hand.

"So maybe color isn't the key in this case," she says. "Bottom line—someone's watching you. They obviously followed you to Ben's house. Did you ever talk to Debbie about that creepy phone call you got?"

"Yeah. And she still blames Ben."

"I told you," she sings. "According to Todd—who's yet to call me after sucking my neck, by the way—Debbie's parents are way determined to find a scapegoat for her accident."

"A scapegoat or the person who did it?"

"Whichever comes first."

"Great," I say. Then I tell her Debbie's theory about the black sedan. "She was kind enough to point out that Ben's aunt drives a car that fits the same description as the one that hit her."

"Don't listen to Debbie. She wears platform shoes and palazzo pants."

"So clearly she's delusional."

"I won't argue there, but I also think she's trying to psyche you out."

"Maybe," I say, hearing my voice shake. "But I saw his aunt's car today. And there was a dent."

"Coincidence?"

"I don't know, but his aunt was really weird. She totally caught me checking out her car."

"Maybe *she's* the one who's watching you."

"Be serious."

"Oh, I'm sorry, do you have a better explanation?"

I nibble my lip, thinking how long it took for Ben to

appear once his aunt let me in. Is it possible that he left the photo?

"Are you sure you don't want me to come over?" Kimmie asks.

"No. I need to think. I need to pack."

"You need some rest," she corrects me.

"That too." I glance in my dresser mirror. There are dark circles beneath my eyes and my hair is a mangy mess. I tug at a strand of blond, noticing how the ends are frayed from being pulled up into a ponytail every day.

Kimmie and I say our good-byes, and I drift off to sleep without even changing out of my clothes or wishing my parents good luck on their trip.

52

WHEN I WAKE UP the following morning to the blare of my alarm clock, I find a note on my bedside table. It's from my mom, telling me how she and Dad came in to my bedroom last night, but I was already asleep.

"We also came in to check on you this morning," my mother wrote, "but you've been so exhausted, we didn't want to wake you."

There are phone numbers and addresses listed for where they'll be and how I can reach them, and promises to call me just as soon as they land.

I crawl out of bed and pull on some clothes, foregoing breakfast in lieu of an extra ten minutes of zoning out in front of the TV. Then I head off to school.

The morning schedule has been slightly adjusted due to the long-awaited assembly, at which Principal Snell lectures the entire student body about the resurgence of pranks over the past couple weeks and the rumors of more yet to come.

"Anyone even thinking about doing any pranking or hazing during their 'academic career' here at Freetown will suffer the consequences," Snell says, banging his fist down hard against the podium. "It will *not* be tolerated. Action *will* be taken."

There's giggling from the audience, including from the row in front of me, where John Kenneally, Davis Miller, and Todd "Neck-Sucking" McCaffrey are seated. They're passing a notebook among themselves. There's a snapshot of Ben taped to a page. Davis draws a knife in one of Ben's hands, while Todd adds a chainsaw to the other. Meanwhile, John Kenneally tries to stifle a laugh as he writes the words "I'd kill to get laid" right above Ben's head.

I bite my lip, wondering if any of them might be behind some of the pranks I've been getting, especially since they're using a photo.

When the assembly is finally over, I dart out of the auditorium to my first block of the day, but before I can get there, Ben stops me.

"We need to talk," he says.

"Not now," I say, trying to move past him.

"Then when?"

"We're done talking, remember?"

"Just give me a few minutes," he insists.

I glance around, noting the crowd of kids going off to their classes, brushing past Ben and bumping against his backpack. Ben breathes through it all, trying to mentally shake off the sensations.

This must really be important.

Debbie stands only a few feet away, outside the computer lab, waiting for Mr. Nadeau to unlock the door so everyone can file in. She folds her arms and stares straight at us.

"How about tonight?" he suggests.

"I won't be around. My parents are away."

"You won't be alone," he says, more of a statement than a question; there's a degree of concern in his voice.

"I'm staying at Kimmie's."

"How about *before* Kimmie's?"

"Before Kimmie's I have to go home and pack."

"And before that?"

"I have plans," I say, meeting his eyes.

Ben nods and studies my face, probably inferring the truth in my lack of details—that "plans" means I'll be busy with Adam.

"Are you free after school, then? I could meet you."

"Where?" I ask, finally succumbing to his persistence.

"I'll find you."

A second later, the final bell rings. I hurry up the stairs, two at a time, just hoping Madame Funkenwilder doesn't give me a detention for coming in late. Luckily, we have a sub. And even luckier is that said sub— appropriately named Ms. Pecker, with her pointed nose, beady eyes, and nest of hair—grants us a free block so long as nobody looks idle, does anything illegal, or mutters a single word. A small price to pay for the time it'll take me to finish the overdue homework I've yet to even start.

After school, I exit the main entrance with Wes and Kimmie at my side. Ben is already waiting for me. I spot his motorcycle parked just beyond the traffic circle.

"Like clockwork," Kimmie says.

"More like a piece of work," Wes corrects. "Do you want us to hang around for a bit?"

"No, thanks. I've already got a ride."

Kimmie tsks-tsks. "You really do have a penchant for self-inflicted torture, don't you?"

"I'm not going with Ben," I clarify. "Adam is driving me home. I'll call you when I get there."

"You'll do better than call me, Miss Chameleon," she says. "You're staying at my house, remember?"

"Right, so once I'm done with Ben, I'll have Adam bring me home to pack and then drop me off at your house. Sound good?"

"More like mildly acceptable, but I guess I'll take it." She gives me a squeeze for luck, and then I make my way over to Ben.

Ben is dressed in a black leather jacket and dark-washed jeans. I try not to notice how amazingly good he looks.

"Can we go someplace private to talk?" he asks.

"I'm actually waiting for someone." I look over my shoulder to make sure that Adam isn't here yet.

Ben follows my gaze and gives a subtle nod, like he fully gets the picture, and like that picture disappoints him.

We end up in the lobby of the auditorium, where I can still keep an eye on the traffic circle outside, but where it's private enough to talk.

"So, what's going on?" he asks, his arms folded.

"With what?"

"I opened your present."

"And?"

"And, what's going on?" he repeats. "How did you know about that? Is this all just some way to get back at me?"

"Get back at you for what?"

"You've been snooping around in my past," he says.

"Ben, I have absolutely no idea what you're talking about."

"Then how did you know about the horse?"

I shake my head, still thoroughly confused. "The horse has some significance for you?"

"Are you trying to tell me that you don't know?"

"Why would I be snooping?"

"You were snooping last night . . . when you came to my house. My aunt told me she saw you checking out her fender."

My face heats up, guilty as charged. I look down at my hands, feeling the pools of sweat begin to form on my palms.

"What were you looking for?" he asks, though it's clear

from his expression that he already knows. His jaw is tense.

"And what was *she* doing spying on *me?*" I volley back. "She must have been sitting in her car, waiting for me to come out of mine. I didn't even see her inside. Was she crouched down by the wheel?"

"She was cleaning out her car. She saw you coming toward hers, and wanted to see what you were up to."

"So then why did she shine her headlights in my face? And why did she rev her motor?"

"I already told you," he says, "there've been a lot of pranks going on around my house, even more now that I'm back in school. My aunt is just being extra protective. This isn't easy for her, you know."

"It isn't easy for any of us."

"It'll be easier if you tell me what you were looking for when you were inspecting my aunt's car."

"Why don't *you* tell *me?*" I ask, suspecting he already knows the answer.

"You saw the dent, didn't you?"

"Is there something you want to tell me about it?"

"I can't believe we're still talking about this. That dent's been there for over two years. Do you honestly think the police didn't already look into it? Do you think that when Debbie went into a coma, I wasn't the first person they came looking for?"

"Then why does Debbie think it was you?"

"Do you really have to ask?"

I shake my head, remembering how Kimmie told me

that Debbie and her family are determined to pin the accident on someone. "So what does all this have to do with my horse sculpture?"

Ben takes a moment, his eyes focused toward the wall instead of on me. "I gave Julie a pendant that looked exactly like the horse you sculpted. The stance, the legs, the head . . . everything. It hung from a chain. She wore it around her neck."

I swallow hard, not really knowing what to say. My skin ices over, and a chill runs down my back.

"Julie was into competitive horseback riding, which is why I bought it for her," he continues. "But on the day we broke up—that day on the cliff—she gave it back to me. She said she didn't want it anymore."

"Ben, I had no idea. I mean, I only did what you suggested," I say, referring to my sculpture. "I went with my impulse, with what I was feeling."

"Well, your impulse led you to create my ex-girlfriend's pendant."

I bite the inside of my cheek, wondering what this all means, what it means that I obviously have this ability, and what it means that I'd sculpt something from Ben's past . . . from the day his girlfriend died.

"I still remember hiking up that mountain with her," he says. "She seemed distracted, like something was definitely wrong. I tried lightening the mood by pretending to trip, finally getting her to giggle a couple times, but I could tell she didn't want to. So she just kept telling me to be careful—"

"Excuse me?" I ask, nearly dropping my books.

"She wanted me to be careful," he explains. "She was afraid I might hurt myself. Only it wasn't me who ended up falling."

My heart races as I put the pieces together inside my head: the sculpture, the words, the giggling. It was Julie's voice I heard that day in the basement, playing in my mind's ear.

"So maybe we should talk about this," Ben says.

"Definitely," I whisper, wondering if he senses it too, how truly alike we are.

"But there's something I have to tell you first."

A moment later, Adam's car pulls into the traffic circle. Ben notices and turns to look. "I guess your ride is here," he says.

"Just tell me," I insist.

"Maybe I've wasted too much time already."

"What's that supposed to mean?"

"Be careful," he whispers. "I think someone might be trying to trick you in some way."

"Is that what you sense? Is that the real reason you've been keeping tabs on me?"

"You have to go," he says. "Your boyfriend's waiting."

"No," I snap, reminded of the photo left on my windshield. "You can't just say something like that. You can't just tell me I'm being tricked and then walk away. Maybe *you're* the one who's tricking me. Maybe you've been tricking me all along."

"I guess it's up to you to decide who you can trust," he says.

"Tell me," I repeat. "Just explain to me what you mean. How is someone trying to trick me? Do you mean all the stuff that's been happening with the photos and the notes? Are they definitely just pranks?"

"I already said everything I needed to."

And with that, Ben turns away and heads out the door.

*T*HERE'S A NUMBING sensation crawling over my skin as I walk to Adam's car. It's sort of like I'm on autopilot, going through the motions of my day, like nothing ever happened.

Even though part of me wants to collapse.

Adam spots me coming toward him and gets out of his car. He opens the passenger-side door and gestures for me to climb inside. He's smiling until he sees my face—my crumbled expression and how I can barely look up from my shoes.

"What's wrong?" he asks.

I get inside and close the door, then flip the visor down to block out the sun. My reflection stares back at me in the mirror.

"Do you want to talk about it?" Adam asks, back inside the car now.

"I want to go," I whisper, gazing down at my lap.

"*Where* do you want to go?"

"Away." I turn the radio up. The blaring buzz of the music helps block out my thoughts—all the questions and all the confusion—and numb me up even more.

Adam begins down the road, taking a bunch of turns and driving us in circles, clearly at a loss for where to go, but it doesn't matter. He raises his voice so I can hear him over the music: "Hungry?"

"Take me to Knead," I say, checking my watch. We've been riding around for at least a half hour.

"What's at Knead?"

"Nothing." I look out the window and watch the rush of pine trees blur together into one long, green line. "No one. That's sort of the point." I rest my forehead against the window, remembering how Spencer said he'd be going to the city to pick up clay supplies today. "We can talk in private."

Without another question, Adam takes us to Knead, probably relieved to finally have a destination. He unlocks the door and flicks on the overhead lights. We end up sitting at one of the tables toward the back. It's already set up for tomorrow morning's class, which tells me that Spencer must have come in today after all.

"So, what's going on?" Adam asks, taking a seat across from me.

I grab a carving tool from the center of the table and twiddle it nervously in my hand. "I think I may have mentioned it before, but my life is sort of intense right now. I don't expect you to understand. I don't even expect you to put up with me."

"Stop," he says, reaching out to touch my forearm. "I wouldn't be here if I didn't want to be."

"I know," I say, venturing to look up at him.

Adam wipes a stray strand of hair from my eyes. "Tell me what's going on. I want to help."

"Why?" I ask, still able to hear Ben's words in my mind's ear, telling me that someone's trying to trick me.

"Because I care about you." He lifts my chin with his finger, forcing me to look at him again.

"You don't think I'm nuts?"

"Actually, I think you're pretty great . . . when you're not being scary, that is."

"*Scary?*"

He pries the carving tool out of my hand and places it out of reach. "Maybe we should keep all sharp objects at a distance," he jokes. "At least until you're in a more cheerful mood."

"Very funny."

"At least it got you laughing."

"I'm sorry," I say. "I don't mean to be all high maintenance. Maybe you should just drop me off at Kimmie's."

"Does this somber mood have something to do with your ex?" he asks.

"I really don't feel like getting into it."

"Then how can I help you?"

"You've already helped," I say. "You brought me here, didn't you?"

"But now you want to go?"

I shrug, not really knowing what I want. I grab a ball of clay from the recycled bin by the sink and begin wedging it out on a workboard. The rhythmic slapping as clay meets wood helps ease the jangling of my nerves, the tension in my muscles. I pound the clay down, grateful for the break in conversation, to simply concentrate on the form and texture of the clay as I work to get all the air bubbles out.

"So there's something I need to tell you," Adam says.

"What is it?" I ask, reaching for a rolling pin to smooth out the lumps.

He hesitates, almost afraid to tell me maybe, but then he finally says it: "I like you."

"I like you too," I say, somewhat confused. I mean, haven't we already been through this before?

"No, I mean I *really* like you." His face is completely serious, like there's so much more going on here than just his mere admiration. "I knew coming here . . . going to school here . . . would be all well and good. I just never imagined I'd like you this much."

"Did you think you *wouldn't* like me?" I ask, thinking back to the first time we met here, at Knead, when I nearly tore his head off at the door.

"Do you mind if I help you with that?" he asks, gesturing to my ball of clay. "I'd really like to learn the wheel."

"Seriously?"

He nods again, and we move over to the wheel station. I sit on the stool and Adam squats down beside me. "You have to keep your hands moist," I say, dipping a sponge into a bin of water and squeezing the liquid out over his fingers.

I throw the clay ball down with a smack, flick the switch that turns on the motor, and press my foot against the pedal, feeling an instant jolt of connectedness—me with my work.

The plate revolves counterclockwise. "Are you ready?" I ask, leaning forward to place my hands over the mound.

Adam positions his hands over mine, and I instantly lose that connected feeling. Still, I try to keep focused, working the sides of the ball upward into the shape of a cone. Adam slides his hands toward my wrists, trying to catch the rhythm as I make the cone grow taller.

"This is a lot tougher than it looks," he says.

His fingers are dry and gritty against my skin. I wring a sponge out over them until water drips down over the plate.

"Your hands really need to become one with the clay," I say.

Adam's breath is at my ear, reminding me of Ben. Actually, this whole scenario reminds me of him—of that day, last September, when we sculpted that pinecone shape. Even that ended up coming true.

I remember how at first I thought it was funny, and sort of random, to be sculpting something with my crush—with Ben—and to have it turn out to be a pinecone. But then later, when Matt took me captive, I remember sitting in his car, seeing the pinecone air freshener that hung from his rearview mirror, and thinking what a coincidence it was.

I'm not even sure I believe in coincidence anymore.

"Am I totally screwing this up?" Adam asks, probably noticing how my hands have stopped moving, and how my mound has lost its center. The bowl-in-process is warped now.

I ease up on the pedal to stop the revolution. Then I straighten the bowl out, blaming my lack of focus—my lack of connectedness—on the clay. "This is why I never use this gray stuff," I explain. "The red clay is so much better. More tooth, better grog."

"*Grog?*"

"Shoptalk." I grin. "It basically just means that it has more grit."

"And grit is good?"

"It's very good. More earthy, less mealy."

"Are you sure you're not talking about worms?"

I smile wider and begin again, bearing my hands down over the mound to form the base.

Adam moves even closer, finally scooting in behind me on the stool. "Is this okay?" His thighs graze my hips.

I clench my teeth, trying to keep focused, trying to keep *his* lack of focus from making me more nervous.

Adam glides his hands up and down my arms as I press my fingers inside the mouth of the bowl to open it up.

I take a deep breath, thinking how this feels so much different from that time with Ben and the pinecone.

Adam presses against me. I can feel the heat of his

chest on my back. And then he kisses me. His lips draw a line from my shoulder to the nape of my neck, completely startling me. I puncture my finger through a wall in the bowl, collapsing the sides.

"No," I whisper, pulling away.

"What's wrong?"

I look down at the bowl, completely broken now. "This just doesn't feel right."

"Oh," he says, as if taken aback. I can hear the disappointment in his voice.

"I think maybe I just need to be alone right now."

"Well, at least let me drive you home."

"Actually, I think I'll stay. I'd like to work for a while."

Adam hesitates, but then grabs his coat.

"Please know that it's not you," I say.

"Yes it is. Because I'm not Ben. And I obviously never will be."

54

*A*FTER ADAM LEAVES and I'm finally alone, part of me's relieved, but I also can't help feeling like something's been lost, too. I glance down at the pottery wheel, knowing that I should probably clean up. The water bin is empty now, and the remnants of my bowl look like they've already started to dry. I go to toss the clay scraps into the recycle bin, when I get an overwhelming sensation that I'm being watched.

I take a step back against the wall and scan the studio. Most of the lights are on in the work area, but they're all off in the back, where there are no windows, making it hard to see. I strain my eyes. At the same moment, a cracking sound comes from the back stairwell.

"Spencer?" I call, checking to see that his work light is shut off too.

When no one answers, I grab a vase and move into the darkness. The light switch that illuminates the back area is several yards away by the kiln. I head in that direction, but then a squeaking noise stops me. It sounds like someone's coming up the back staircase, like rubber-soled sneakers against metal steps.

I duck into a corner, behind the tubs of glaze, hoping the darkness will hide me.

"Camelia?" a male voice whispers. "Is that you?"

My cell phone rings in my pocket. I reach for it, but the phone slips from my grasp and clanks against the floor. My heart starts hammering inside my chest.

I peer toward the exit door, wondering if I should try to run. Meanwhile, a shadow moves along the wall, getting larger with each approaching step.

"Where are you?" the voice whispers.

The vase still clenched in my hand, I ready myself to fight. But then the lights flash on, stinging my eyes. I blink a bunch of times, trying to regain focus.

Finally I'm able to see the blur of someone standing only a few feet away. The vase falls from my grip with a crash. A cold hard scream tears from my throat.

55

$\mathcal{S}$ TANDING ONLY A FEW feet away, Ben looks like I've scared him too. His face is white. His lips are parted in surprise.

"How did you get in here?" I shout.

"The front door was wide open. Spencer was busy unloading boxes when I came inside. I don't even think he saw me."

"What are you doing here?"

"I was looking for you, but you weren't working up here, so I went downstairs. The next thing I knew, Spencer was gone, the door was locked. I couldn't get the back door open either, so I ran downstairs to see if there might be another way out, but then I heard you guys come in and I didn't want to interrupt."

"So you were spying on me?"

"I was looking for you," he says again. "I shouldn't have walked away before."

I clench my fists, suddenly noticing the boxes of clay on the floor outside Spencer's workroom. Is it possible that Ben's telling the truth? Or did he follow Adam and me here, breaking in through the back somehow?

"How did you know where to find me?" I ask.

"It was the only place left. I already went by your house, the coffee shop, and that ice-cream place where you and your friends like to go. I thought that maybe, even if you weren't here, I could check your work schedule."

"Well, I'm done talking. You had your chance." I grab my coat, readying to leave. But then the door whips open.

It's Adam.

"Camelia?" he gasps, all out of breath. "I heard you scream. . . ." It takes him a second to put the pieces together: my troubled expression and the broken vase at my feet.

He moves a bit closer, finally able to see Ben.

And then he lunges toward him.

"Adam, no!" I shout, grabbing his arm to hold him back.

"Did he hurt you?" Adam asks. "Did he lay even a single finger on you?"

"Adam, stop!" I'm still gripping his arm.

Ben moves behind a worktable to avoid being touched.

Adam stands opposite him. A satisfied smirk creeps across his lips. "What are you doing here?" he asks.

"I could ask you the same," Ben says.

Adam slides his arm around my shoulder. "Just making sure that my girlfriend is safe."

I take a step back, so Adam's arm falls limp. "Do you two know each other?" I ask.

"I told you that you were being tricked," Ben says.

"Maybe *you're* the one tricking her."

"Adam and I go way back," Ben explains. "We used to be friends, but then he betrayed our friendship when he started seeing my girlfriend behind my back."

"She wasn't your girlfriend," Adam corrects. "She only felt sorry for you. That's why she didn't break up with you right away."

"You mean Julie?" I ask.

"He killed her," Adam says. "He pushed her off a cliff and left her for dead."

"You don't know what you're talking about," Ben snaps. "I stayed with Julie. I got help right away—"

"Which one was it?" Adam asks.

Ben doesn't answer. Instead he looks at me, trying to see if I believe him.

"What's going on?" I whisper.

"Do you know how long it took me to get over her?" Adam continues, still focused on Ben.

"Is that why you came here?" I ask him. "Is this some sort of payback?" I shake my head, thinking about his persistence with me—how he wouldn't take no for an answer.

Adam's eyes soften as he looks into my face. "I don't expect you to understand. And I know it doesn't look good, but I meant it when I said that I care about you. I just never expected to care so much."

"I trusted you," I say, hating myself for having opened up to him.

"I care about you," he repeats. "You *can* trust me." Adam reaches for my hand. This time I let him take it, almost wishing that I could be like Ben and read the truth just by touching him.

Ben moves to take my other hand, but stops just shy of my wrist.

"How does it feel," Adam asks him, pulling me close, "to have someone you love taken from you?"

I try to pull away, but Adam's grip on my hand tightens. "Please," he insists. "Just hear me out. I never wanted to hurt you."

"Maybe you should go," Ben says, smacking Adam's hand away.

Adam responds by shoving Ben into a worktable. Tools go flying. Ben's head snaps back; he falls down hard against a large ceramic mold.

"Are you okay?" I ask Ben.

Ben dives into Adam's midsection. They land with a loud hard crash that causes the entire floor to rumble and shake.

"No!" I shout, trying to pull Ben off him.

Still, Adam rebounds, pounding his fist into Ben's jaw. Ben lets out a grunt but remains straddled on top of him.

Adam grapples to break free, to jab his fingers into Ben's eyes and swing at the sides of his face. But Ben grabs Adam's hands and pins them under his knees. "I wouldn't move if I were you." He grips Adam's neck, stopping just shy of applying pressure. His eyes are filled with rage.

"No!" I shout again, knowing that Ben is on the brink

of losing control. The muscles in his fingers are taut, as if ready to clench.

Adam's eyes water, brimming with fear.

Unable to pull Ben off him, I search the floor for my phone—I want to call the police, but I can't find it anywhere. Meanwhile, the studio phone extension is off the base. I press the locator button, only to discover that the receiver's locked up in Spencer's office.

"Don't do this," I shout; tears fill my eyes. I grab a ceramic plate and whack it against Ben's back.

Still, he doesn't move. It's like there's a power struggle inside him: something's telling him to walk away, but he can't seem to move.

"Please," I beg Ben. I kneel down at his side, noticing the sudden look of fear in his eyes, as if maybe he's scared too.

I place my palms down over his hands. It forces him to look at me—to cross back over and come to his senses.

Ben finally backs away and Adam moves to sit up.

Standing now, Ben searches my eyes as if checking for my reaction. All I feel is fear.

"I'm sorry," he says, though I can't tell who he's directing his apology to. He looks at Adam and then back at me, as if completely at a loss for what could have happened.

"Are you okay?" I ask Adam.

Adam manages a nod, but his eyes look red and puffy. Meanwhile, Ben moves even farther away, finally fleeing out the door.

56

June 19, 1984

Dear Diary,

I tried to end my life two nights ago. I slit my wrists, watched the blood trickle out for a few seconds, and then panicked and wrapped the cuts up with my bedsheet.

I've been wearing long sleeves to cover the scars. I've been wearing a smile to mask the pain.

Alexia

57

*A*FTER THE INCIDENT at Knead, I find myself standing in the lobby of the town library, not really knowing where else to go. Or what to do.

Adam left the pottery studio shortly after Ben. I offered to call him an ambulance, but he wasn't interested, saying that I still needed to hear him out; that he never imagined falling for me; and that, despite their fight, Ben could **never hurt** him again.

I didn't point out that Ben could have done much *more* than hurt him. He could have taken his life.

Once I found my cell phone, I too ended up bolting from the studio. I checked my caller ID to see who had phoned earlier. It was my parents. They'd left me a message saying they'd arrived safely in Detroit and asking me where I was.

I know I should call them back. I know that Kimmie must be wondering about me too. I just need a little silence right now.

I gaze out the library window at the street. It's a little before six, but it already looks well past nine. The pavement glistens with a layer of frost.

The thing is, I know how I should be feeling about Ben right now. I know it should be nothing more than pure anger mixed with fear. And I *do* feel those things. But there's a sadness too, almost like death. And I'm not talking about the death of our relationship, or any of the residual feelings that still might be lingering. I'm talking about the sadness I feel for Ben. I mean he's worked so hard at isolating himself and not touching anyone, and then this happens.

He could have killed someone.

I close my eyes, trying to sort through the last two hours. I just can't believe that Adam would go to so much trouble to find Ben and try to make him jealous—more than two years later.

But maybe in some small and twisted way, it sort of makes sense. For Ben, coming to Freetown and trying public school again was like a new beginning, a fresh start—the perfect opportunity for Adam to crush him.

"It's about freakin' time," Kimmie says, when I finally dial her number from the library breezeway. "I've been waiting all afternoon for you. I thought Adam was dropping you off."

"Sorry," I say, proceeding to give her the entire scoop, including the stuff about Julie's pendant.

"Why is it that all the hot ones have to be megawatt assholes?" she asks, referring to Adam. "So, you know that's why he landed himself a job at Knead. When he got to town, he must have found out about you and your connection to Ben."

"Well, that wouldn't have been very hard."

"No kidding, in a small town like this . . . ? Yesterday, when I went through the checkout at Munchies, the owner—that Harrison guy—asked me if I was still seeing Todd. I didn't even think he knew my name, never mind the sordid details of my love life."

"Don't you mean your *lust* life?"

"Don't remind me. I feel like total trampage. I mean, what was I thinking by letting Todd hickey me like that?"

"You were thinking it might distract your parents from their feuding. Or at least that's why Frannie let Joey plant a big fat hickey on her for the season finale of *Totally Teen Princess*."

"Todd finally called me, by the way. About an hour ago."
"And?"

"And he asked to see me again, but I told him no."

"Good for you."

"Better for my neck. And speaking of necks . . . will Adam press charges against Ben?"

"I doubt it. He seemed more worried about what I might think of him."

"Okay, so maybe he's only a deci-watt asshole."

"Still an asshole."

"Where are you, by the way? You're supposed to be staying with me, remember?"

"I'm sort of on the verge of a major breakdown."

"Because of Ben?"

"Because here I've been defending him all along, and I just witnessed him almost kill someone."

"But he *didn't* kill him. You stopped him. As twisted as it sounds, it's almost like he needs you. Like you need each other."

I let out a breath and watch the way it steams up the window—ironically, in the shape of a heart. "I just feel like I should have seen this coming. I mean, even earlier at the studio, before Ben showed up, I could sense Adam wanted to tell me something. He kept saying how much he liked me. How he never imagined feeling that way."

"Yes, but you *did* see this coming," Kimmie corrects me. "At least part of it. I mean, I can't even believe I'm saying this, but your sculpture helped predict this."

"The horse," I whisper, picturing my tall dark sculpture as a pendant on Julie's necklace.

"It's pretty bitchin', wouldn't you say? I mean, that kind of foresight can take you places. It can take *us* places."

"I guess." I sigh, not really wanting to get into it.

"So, what about all the pranks? Do you seriously think it was Adam calling you and leaving all those notes and photos?"

"That wouldn't make any sense. It wasn't me, after all, that he was trying to get back at. I was merely a casualty in the process."

"A casualty who needs her friends around her. Where are you? I'll thief my mom's car keys and come pick you up."

"I'm not even packed yet."

"You don't need to pack. You can borrow my stuff."

"We're not exactly the same size," I say, cringing at the thought of having to wear one of her chain-adorned skirts or the top with the latex corset. "Plus, it'll only take me a little while to stuff a few things into a bag."

"Then I can pick you up?"

"Fair enough. I'll call you when I'm ready."

"If I don't call you sooner. I refuse to wait around this time, Chameleon. Got it?"

"Loud and clear."

After we hang up, I dial my mom's cell phone. "Are you okay?" she asks. "I've been trying to reach you."

"I'm fine," I lie.

"Are you with Kimmie?"

I mumble a yes and then add to my lie, telling her that Kimmie and I have been far too busy mall-ratting to even think about answering phone calls. At first I feel bad, but then I hear the relief in her voice, and I know I've done the right thing.

"How's Aunt Alexia?" I ask, eager to switch the subject.

"It's still early, but we're making real progress. We met with her therapist this afternoon."

"And?"

"And I'll have a lot to tell you when your dad and I get home. So I'll give you a call tomorrow?"

"Okay," I say, almost wishing that I could just be

honest with her. My eyes well up and sting at the corners. "I gotta go," I say, hearing a slight quiver in my voice. "Kimmie's waiting for me."

Somehow I make it to the end of the conversation without losing it completely. And then I allow myself to crouch down in the corner, behind the newspaper machine, and cry until my eyes feel swollen and raw.

58

W HEN I GET HOME, the light on the answering machine is blinking. I push PLAY, almost startled by the voice: "This message is for Mr. and Mrs. Hammond. This is Denise Beady, the school counselor at the high school. I was wondering if we might schedule a meeting to discuss some things. Could one of you please call me just as soon as you get this message?"

She goes on to leave both her office and cell phone numbers; then she reiterates most of what she already said, adding in all the dates and times that she's available to meet. But I can't really listen anymore. I smack the DELETE button, accidentally knocking the phone receiver to the floor.

The mantel clock in the living room chimes seven o'clock. It's a familiar sound, but now, in the solitude of the house, it sends shivers down my spine.

I move quickly through the hallway to my bedroom,

anxious to pull together a few things and have Kimmie come pick me up. I click on my light. And spot it right away.

My sweatshirt. The one Ben accidentally took from my bedroom, the one he supposedly left in my homeroom at school. It's propped up on my pillow, positioned so I can see it.

Someone has written over the chest. At first I can't quite process what it says. I blink a few times, as if maybe it'll go away. But it doesn't. And the words don't. The message stares back at me in thick black letters: YOU'RE DEAD.

I take a step closer, flashing back to the message on the bulkhead doors, suddenly realizing that someone was in here—that it's possible they never left.

A second later, a door slams somewhere in the house, followed by the sound of my cell phone ringing. With jittery fingers I reach into my pocket and check the caller ID. It's blocked, but I click the phone on anyway: "Hello?"

No one answers.

"Hello," I repeat, louder this time.

"You're dead!" a voice screeches, then breaks into a menacing laugh.

"Who is this?"

The laughter continues, and then the phone goes silent, like the call was dropped, or maybe the person hung up. I flip the phone closed, open it back up, and dial 9-1-1, but the call doesn't go through. It's still silent on the other end.

Assuming I lost the signal, I grab the phone in my

room, but I don't get a dial tone. "Hello?" I say into the receiver, wondering if someone's on the other end. I click the phone on and off a bunch of times without any luck. It's as if the phone line has been cut.

Floorboards creak somewhere in the house. I snag a bookend off my shelf and peer down the hallway toward the kitchen. I know I left the kitchen light on, but someone has turned it off.

I open my door a little farther so that the light from my room illuminates the hallway. Slowly I move toward the kitchen, my heart pounding with each step—so loud I can hear it in my ears. Finally in the kitchen, I flick on the light.

Everything appears normal, like I never left it. I turn on the light in the living room as well. That appears okay too.

I take a deep breath, feeling my stomach lurch. I trade the bookend for a knife from the drawer, then close my eyes and silently count to ten.

A moment later, a breaking sound comes from downstairs. The noise cuts right through my bones and I let out a gasp. I open the basement door as carefully as possible, but it lets out a high-pitched whine. "Hello?" I call.

I flip on the stairwell light and wait a few moments, listening. There's just the hum of the refrigerator from somewhere behind me.

Still gripping the knife, I move down the stairs. "Is someone down here?" I ask.

The basement light is just out of reach. I take a couple

more steps, feeling a chill in the air, wondering if my dad forgot to close up the corner window again. I peer in that direction, noticing a flame flickering on my worktable, as though from a candle. Its light casts a shadow on the wall.

Adrenaline courses through my veins; I can feel it in my arms as I grip the knife tighter and turn on the light. I move closer to my worktable. The candle illuminates a series of snapshots propped up against various bowls I've made. They're pictures of me and pictures of Ben, though we're not together: it's either me alone, or Ben by himself.

It takes me a moment to notice the writing across each snapshot. Someone's scribbled a word over each of the photos, until the message comes together: TILL DEATH DO US PART.

The knife drops from my grip. A long-winded scream peals from my throat. And then someone's hand covers my mouth.

59

WITH SOMEONE'S HAND still cupped over my mouth, I try to step back, but the person doesn't budge. And so I bite down into the skin of his hand until my jaw aches—and until I'm finally released. I grab a carving knife from my worktable and spin around.

Only to find Ben.

"What are you doing here? How did you get in?"

"Shhh," he says. "You left the front door open."

"No. I didn't." I know I locked the front door promptly behind me.

"We're not alone," he whispers, gesturing toward the photos. "Someone called me tonight."

"*Who* called you?"

"I don't know," he says, keeping his voice low. He looks over his shoulder toward the staircase. "You need to come with me."

"I'm not going anywhere until you tell me what you're

266

talking about. Until you tell me what you're doing here."

"I'll explain everything. Just come with me now."

"No," I say, glancing back at the photos.

Ben follows my gaze. "You can't possibly think it was me who left those pictures."

"How long have you been here?" I ask, assuming that it was he who made that door slam upstairs, that it was his footsteps that made the floorboards creak.

"Someone called me," he says again.

I shake my head. "You have to go."

"No." His jaw locks. "I'm not going anywhere." He goes to grab my arm, but I push him back.

He comes at me again, slowly at first. But then he takes my arms, squeezes the knife right out of my hand, and restrains me from behind.

I stomp on his feet and bite his hand again. He lets out a wail, loosening his grip. I kick at his shin—hard—plunging the heel of my boot against his bone. He continues to try to overpower me, to grab my arm and lead me toward the back of the basement, by the bulkhead exit. "Please," he insists, trying to keep control of his breath.

I twist my arm, forcing him to release me. Then I grab a pot off my shelf and bash it over his head. Ben lets out a moan before going down. The pot smashes to bits on the floor.

I hurry up the stairs, nearly tripping at the top and suddenly noticing that the phone in the kitchen is on the floor, where I'd dropped it before. I pick it up. The line-in-use light is on, indicating that it's been off the hook. For all this time. It must have clicked on when it landed against the tile.

I click it off and then turn it back on to get a dial tone, surprised when I hear a beeping sound, like someone's trying to dial. I turn it off, then on again, and reposition the receiver against my cheek, thinking maybe I brushed against it by accident, that maybe I hit the redial button.

But then I hear a voice: "My name is Camelia Hammond. And my ex-boyfriend wants to kill me. He's broken into my house."

My mouth quivers open, completely confused. The receiver still pressed against my ear, I peer down the hallway toward my room.

"What is your address?" the operator asks.

"I live at 222 Seersucker Road, Freetown, Massachusetts," the female voice says.

"We're sending someone over right away," the operator continues. "Just stay on the line with me."

"I can't," she says, between tears.

"Why not? Can he hear you? Where are you in the house? Where is he?"

"I'm in my bedroom." She sniffles. "I don't know where he is. In the basement, maybe."

Slowly, I move down the hallway toward my room, listening as the 9-1-1 operator instructs the girl to try to relax. I edge the door to my bedroom open.

Debbie Marcus is there, crouched on the floor; the phone receiver is pressed against her cheek. She clicks the phone off, a smug smile across her freckled lips. "I was hoping to leave before you saw me."

Dressed all in black—from ski hat to snow boots—she

lets out a sigh. "But I couldn't get the damned phone to work." She tosses the receiver to the floor, and it rings not two seconds later.

"Why bother getting it?" She rolls her eyes. "The police will be here any second, which is why I'd better go. Thanks for not locking the basement window, by the way. It sure makes for an easy break-in."

"What are you doing?" I ask, already putting some of the pieces together—the photos, the weird phone calls, and the message written across the bulkhead doors. . . ." Did you do that?" I ask, gesturing to my sweatshirt behind her.

"Who else?" She yawns. "I knew it was yours, and I was there when Ben left it in your homeroom that day."

"Why would you do this?"

"Are you serious?" She laughs, her apple cheeks puffing up as she smiles. "Ben's stalking you, remember?"

"*You're* stalking me."

"Correction: I'm only making it *look* like you're getting stalked. And I must say, it's too bad it had to come to all this. I thought you would've been smart enough to alert the authorities, or at least your parents, way before this— more like around the time I left you that shrine photo. But no, you had to be all stubborn and independent."

"What are you talking about?"

"Ben doesn't belong here," she says through gritted teeth. Her steel blue eyes look fierce and feral. "And I have a feeling that after tonight, the police will agree with me."

269

"After tonight?"

"So it'll go down like this," she begins. "You came home tonight to pack, heard some funny noises, found some scary things, only to discover that Ben had broken into your house. And so you dialed 9-1-1, which is the phone call you just heard." She motions to the receiver with her glove-covered hand. "I'll leave out the window before the police arrive, and you can tell them everything."

"What I'll tell them is how crazy you are, how you plotted this whole thing just to frame Ben."

"Prove it. I have an alibi for tonight. I'm at the movie theater." She flashes me a ticket. "Plus, let's face it, who are the police going to believe—Killer Ben; you, who love him; or me, victim of a coma?"

"You called him to come here, didn't you?" I ask, remembering how Ben mentioned someone phoned him.

"Damn straight I did. I had to get him here at just the right time. I had to be all mysterious by blocking the call and changing my voice. I told him that you were home alone, and that he'd better get here if he wanted to see you alive again. I even opened the front door so he could just walk in. Pretty savvy, no?" she asks, tucking a few stray curls back in place beneath her hat. "Even savvier was planning this whole thing. The only snag was your nosy neighbor. After I wrote that message on the bulkhead, I went back to my car all stoked over a job well done, but then I spotted some old guy sitting on his front porch, looking in my direction. It totally freaked me out, so I ended up going back and washing the whole thing off, which is why I called you that night. I wanted to make sure you saw it, or at least that you got the message, so to speak." She laughs.

I shake my head, amazed at how passive she looks, like none of this even fazes her—like she has zero conscience at all.

"Everything really fell into place," she says. "Especially when I overheard you in the hallway today, telling Ben that your parents were away, and that you were coming back here tonight, alone. But then that stupid phone." She gestures to the extension. "If it had actually worked one of the first fifteen times I tried to call out, I'd be out of here. You never would have seen me. You'd totally believe that Ben was the one stalking you this entire time, am I right? Touché with knocking him out, by the way. I heard it all the way upstairs."

"I can't believe you did this."

"I did it for your own good—for everyone's good. Ben doesn't belong here. It's because of him that my grandfather's dead."

"That's not true."

A moment later, police sirens sound in the distance.

"I gotta go," Debbie says, moving toward the window.

"No!" I shout, grabbing her forearm.

Debbie jerks away, but I'm able to snatch her arm back. I go to pull her into the room, but she grabs a picture frame off my shelf and jabs the glass corner into my wrist. A shooting pain ripples up my arm and I have to let go.

Debbie draws the windowpane up and straddles one leg over the ledge. I take a wide stance, angling my body against a bookcase for support. The sirens grow louder, just around the corner now. I lunge at Debbie, digging my fingernails into the fabric of her coat and dragging her off the sill, back into the room. She tumbles onto the floor.

I pin her there, straddling her back and holding her arms down against the floor so she can't move. But still she kicks me. The heel of her boot jabs into the small of my back, sending a searing pain up my spine. I topple off her back. Debbie gets up and kicks me in the gut. I sputter and wince, but still I don't give up. I reach for her leg, but she's able to break free. She snatches a pair of scissors from my desk and positions them high above her head.

"Maybe Ben stabbed you with a pair of scissors while he was here," she whispers. Her eyes are wide and searing.

I position my arms over my head to protect myself. At the same moment, I see Debbie fly backward against the bookcase. Ben rips the scissors out of her hands and tosses them to the floor, out of reach.

He holds her in place using the sweatshirt from my bed as a buffer between them, so he doesn't have to touch her—so he doesn't have to risk losing control all over again. Meanwhile, three police cruisers pull up in front of my house with a screech. I sit back on my heels, grateful that the trickery is finally over, but feeling horrible that I ever suspected Ben was a part of it; that, once again, I doubted him.

60

*I*T'S BEEN FOUR DAYS since the incident at my house, and I still haven't gotten a full night's sleep. I'm sitting at the Press & Grind with Kimmie and Wes, trying to caffeine-and-sugar myself awake so that I won't nod off this afternoon—so that maybe I can get a normal dose of shut-eye tonight.

"I still can't believe Debbie," Wes squawks. "I mean, talk about crazy. She puts the nutter in butter."

"Excuse me?" Kimmie asks; her Pepto-pink lips bunch up in confusion.

"Nutter Butters," Wes explains. "The world's trippiest cookie . . . ?"

"Whatever," she says, rolling her eyes.

The ironic part of this whole Debbie-prankster thing is that she worked so hard at getting Ben to go away. But now she's the one who's gone.

Since no one was seriously hurt, and since my parents

273

knew about Debbie's history with the coma and her grand-father's death, Mom insisted that we not press charges. Dad agreed. Instead, Debbie's parents pulled her out of school, in hopes that she'll be able to get some much-needed perspective, not to mention a bit of counseling.

As soon as my parents heard the news about Debbie and the break-in, they got the first flight home.

"I feel really bad about that," I tell Kimmie and Wes. "This was my mom's opportunity to make real progress with her sister."

"Stop guilting yourself," Kimmie says. "It's our job to screw things up for our parents. Just look at me and Nate. If we'd never been born, my parents would probably still be together."

"Since when are you the poster child for self-pity?" Wes asks, through a mustache of cappuccino froth.

"It's not like my dad didn't say so himself."

Not so surprisingly, Kimmie's parents have decided to separate for a while. Her dad's already renting an apart-ment in the city, with promises to see Kimmie and Nate on the weekends. "My life sucks goat cheese," she says, banging her head against the table.

"Well, let's hope that goat cheese is organic," Wes says. "Remember when Camelia's mom told us they let pus leak into the regular stuff. And I doubt you'd want to suck pus?"

"You're sick," Kimmie tells him.

"Just look on the bright side," he continues. "At least your dad isn't leaving dirty magazines all over the house for you to find. Underneath your pillow, in your gym bag, tucked beneath your place mat at dinner . . ."

"And tell me, oh wise one, why would that side be brighter? Maybe I could use a little dirty distraction."

"What does your mom say about all that dirt?" I ask him.

"Mom's a mouse, even Dad calls her that. If you're not listening closely enough, you won't even hear her squeak."

"Honestly, I don't know how that woman stays with him," Kimmie says. "I think *she* needs a shrink."

"Yeah well, maybe she's not the only one."

"Are you referring to *me?*" she asks him.

He shakes his head and looks away, his face all sullen and pensive.

"Um, Earth to Wes," Kimmie sings.

"Don't worry about it." He forces a half-smile. "I think maybe the coffee-grind fumes are starting to get to me. Does anyone else feel bold and nutty?"

"You know you can talk to us," I say, wondering if the pressure at home is starting to get a little too intense for him.

"I know," he says, choosing instead to make fun of Kimmie's 1960s pillbox hat.

Kimmie and I exchange a look, knowing full well that he's not giving us the full story, but that he clearly doesn't want to elaborate.

Instead, I tell them about the situation with my aunt: how she told my mother she's been hearing voices whenever she paints.

"Seriously?" Kimmie asks. "So this power of yours might actually be a hereditary bonus."

"Like having nice hair?" Wes says, running his fingers over his thickly lacquered coif.

I nod. "Except they don't exactly think of it as a power—more like that she's crazy."

"Which would mean they'd probably think you're crazy too," Kimmie says.

"Or maybe not. Maybe telling them about me might help Aunt Alexia. My parents could think of her supposed psychosis in a whole new way."

"Are you really ready to take that chance?" she asks.

I sink back in my seat, knowing that I'm not—not yet, at least. My mom, especially, was hurt that I didn't say anything, once again, about all the pranks going on. I really don't feel like adding to the list of things I neglected to tell her.

"Bottom line," Kimmie says, "you need to talk to your aunt."

"Agreed," Wes says. "And I'd like to be a fly on the wall when you do."

"I know," I say, wondering if I can convince my mom to let me go with her the next time she travels to Detroit, which is supposedly in a few weeks.

"Were your parents super mad?" Kimmie asks.

"More like super disappointed, but Dad tried to smooth things over, telling Mom about the heart-to-heart we'd had in the parking lot of Taco Bell when I hinted about what was happening."

"Your dad must be heartbroken about Adam," Kimmie says. "I guess it's safe to assume he won't be your dad's future son-in-law."

"Adam is the tricky part in this whole funked-up situation." After the whole blowout, he wrote me a letter. I pull it from my pocket and slide it across the table at them:

Dear Camelia,

I know you won't talk to me right now, but I need to tell you my side of things. It's true that I came to Freetown to try to get back at Ben. I wanted him to know what it feels like to have someone he cares about taken from him, just like he took Julie from me. I know that sounds messed up, but like I said before I never imagined falling for you the way I did.

The plan was stupid. I was stupid. And I'm embarrassed to even have to own up to it now. I hope one day you can forgive me.

I've quit Knead, by the way. It's your place, not mine. But I'm still staying here at the community college. You have my number. I hope you'll use it. I hope one day you'll even be able to forgive me.

Love always,
Adam

"Oh my freaking word," Kimmie blurts.

"You know what I want to know?" Wes asks. "How did he even know where to find Ben? And how did he know you guys were an item last fall?"

"The same way people here found out about Ben's past," I say. "People talk. Rumors spread."

"And losers listen," Kimmie adds. "I mean, obviously Ben was a celebrity in his hometown, or so to speak. The boy probably couldn't even piss in private without someone knowing the color of his briefs. If they are indeed briefs . . . *are* they, Camelia?" She shoots me an evil grin.

"I wouldn't know."

She makes a grimace, clearly disappointed.

"So, are you going to forgive Adam?" Wes asks.

"Or shall it be the dark and dangerous Touch Boy?"

"Do you honestly think that going back to Touch Boy would be a rational decision for our dear Chameleon?" Wes asks her.

"Love isn't rational," she argues. "It's instinctive."

"Well, instinct tells me that I'll know what to do when that time comes."

"Just be sure to keep me posted," Wes says. "Otherwise, I'll be forced to have to deal with my own drama. And, honestly, what fun would that be?"

I look away, thinking about all the loose strands in my life—all the big questions I have yet to answer. "Not very fun at all," I agree.

61

*A*FTER COFFEE WITH Kimmie and Wes, I head to Knead, hoping some work on the wheel might serve as a diversion to my otherwise complicated life. Spencer's there, and he's not alone. It seems he's already hired someone to fill Adam's spot.

Svetlana Stepankov is as tall as she is beautiful, with long and loopy almond brown hair, wide violet eyes, and angular cheeks.

Spencer introduces us, explaining how it'll be my job in the upcoming weeks to show Svetlana the ropes, i.e. to teach her how to fire, how to pull and clean greenware, how to glaze, do the register, set up for classes, and center on the wheel.

"It's nice to meet you," I say, unable to avoid sneaking a peek at the overwhelming cleavage that oozes from her blouse, and the ballerina tattoo that adorns said ooze.

"Yes," she says, all smiles.

"Are you new to the area? How did you find out about this place?"

"Yes," she repeats.

"She doesn't have much experience," Spencer says, like I couldn't have figured that out already, "but I think she'll do wonders for the store. Just talk slowly." He hands me an English–Russian dictionary.

Needless to say, it's pretty apparent why Spencer hired her, but I don't care, because at least this means he'll stop flirting with me, and maybe I'll finally be able to leave all drama at the door.

While he resumes showing Svetlana around (and admiring the dancing ballerina as he does so), I throw a ball of clay onto my spinning wheel, eager to create something great.

But then the door jingles open.

It's Ben.

"Hey," he says. There's a bandage over his temple from when I clobbered him in the basement.

"Hey," I wave, knowing that I should probably run in the other direction. But instead I remain on my stool.

"So, I just wanted to say hello," he says, walking across the studio toward me.

I look behind me for Spencer and Svetlana, but they must be downstairs.

"How have you been?" he asks.

"Not very well, actually," I have to admit.

"Yeah," he says. "Me neither." He looks as lost as I feel. His eyes are tired; his skin is sallow. He can't stop fidgeting in his pockets.

"So, I wouldn't blame you if you never wanted to see again," he continues.

"Are you leaving?" I ask, feeling myself stand, feeling my eyes well up at the mere idea of him going away again.

He shrugs. "I just thought that maybe—"

"Are you leaving?" I repeat, cutting him off, eager for the answer. My container of sculpture tools topples to the floor.

Ben takes my hands. The clay is moist and slippery between our palms. "You're here," he whispers, his eyes tearing up too. "So how could I leave?"

I resist the urge to wilt into his embrace, knowing that this probably isn't rational, but it's definitely instinctive.

"So, we should probably discuss your power of psychometry," he says. "Not to mention mine . . . what you can do, what I can do—what I'm capable of. I'd die if I ever hurt you."

"You'd never hurt me. I know that now."

"Well, you do realize we have a ton to talk about."

"And you do realize you're touching me right now."

He nods and moves closer. His breath is warm against my ear: "And this time I don't ever want to let go."

I look up into his face, noticing how he's started to sweat, and how he's trying his best to control his breath. "Well, I don't really feel like talking right now," I say.

"Neither do I." Ben runs his lips along the length of my neck. And then he kisses me full on the mouth, making my legs feel wobbly and weak.

I kiss him back, resisting the urge to jump into his

arms or tackle him onto the floor. He tastes like honey and sea salt.

Ben slides his hands up my back, beneath my sweatshirt, lingering at my waist. His touch is warm and tender.

My pulse races. My head starts to spin. And all I can think of is that maybe Kimmie was right. Maybe in some weird and twisted way, Ben and I really do need each other.

"For always," he says, as though reading my mind. "For always," I repeat. I draw him closer, and feel his heart beat against my chest.

Acknowledgments

Many thanks to my agent, Kathryn Green, for her invaluable guidance and advice; to my editor, Jennifer Besser, who always asks just the right questions. *Always.* And to Emily Schultz, who helped me delve even deeper.

A special thanks goes to fellow young adult author Stacy DeKeyser, who read pieces of *Deadly Little Lies* during the drafting stage, and who offered insightful feedback.

I'm forever grateful for the support and encouragement of friends and family members—you know who you are. Thanks also to the online community of young adult authors I've befriended over the years, many of whom I've met through yanovelists, YAWRITER, at "the Pub," and/or through The Girlfriends' Cyber Circuit.

And lastly, to my readers, what else can I say except Thank you? Thank you times a kajillion. I am so very truly grateful for your support, encouragement, and continuous enthusiasm for my work.

Look for the next book
in the Touch series,

DEADLY LITTLE GAMES

DEADLY LITTLE GAMES

WHEN I CLOSE MY EYES I can picture his mouth. The way his top lip is slightly fuller than the bottom.

The chapped skin on his lower lip.

And how the corners of his mouth turn upward, even when he's trying to look serious.

My fingers completely saturated with clay, I continue to sculpt the image, remembering that night in front of my house, when I just knew he wanted to kiss me.

It was one of our last dates, and we were sitting in his car during that awkward moment when you're not exactly sure what happens next. Staring at my mouth, Adam leaned in. My blood stirred, and my hands turned cold.

But I didn't kiss him.

I looked away, and his kiss landed on my cheek.

Is it possible that subconsciously I'm regretting that moment?

I open my eyes a couple of minutes later. My sculpture looks eerily real. I touch the chalky surface of the lips, almost able to feel his breath between my fingertips.

"Ten more minutes," Ms. Mazur announces, alerting us to the end of pottery class.

I clear my throat and sit back on my stool, wondering if the heat I feel is visible on my face. I glance around at the other students working away on their sculptures and suddenly feel self-conscious. Because all I've sculpted during this entire ninety-minute block is Adam's mouth.

Adam, who just happens to be my boyfriend Ben's biggest enemy.

Adam, who I'm no longer even interested in.

Adam, who despite the three-hundred-plus other confusing reasons why I shouldn't be giving him a second thought, I've been thinking about all day.

I close my eyes again. The image of Adam's mouth is still alive in my mind—the way his lips were slightly parted that night, and the tiny scar that cuts across the bottom lip, maybe from when he fell as a kid. I try to imagine what he would say if he knew what I was doing.

Would he suspect that I was interested in him?

Would he think it's weird that I remember so much detail about that moment?

Would he tell Ben what I was up to?

I take a deep breath and try my best to focus on the answers. But the only words that flash across my mind, the ones I can't seem to shake, don't address the questions at all.

"You deserve to die," I whisper, then suddenly realize I've said the words aloud.

"*Excuse me?*" my friend Kimmie says. She's sitting right beside me.

"Nothing." I try to shrug it off, adding a dimple to Adam's chin.

"Not *nothing*. You just told me that I deserve to be maggot feed."

"Not maggot feed, just—"

"Dead!" she snaps. Her pale blue eyes, outlined with thick black rings of eye pencil, widen in disbelief.

"Forget it," I say, glancing up at Ms. Mazur, sitting at her desk at the front of the room. "I don't know why I said that. Just daydreaming, I guess."

"Daydreaming about my death?"

"Forget it," I repeat.

"Are you sure you aren't just still mad that I wouldn't let you borrow my vintage fishnet leggings?"

"More like I didn't *want* to borrow them," I say, taking note of her getup du jour: a fringed, fitted Roaring Twenties dress, and a couple of extra-long beaded necklaces that dangle onto the table.

"Even though they would've looked totally hot paired with that cable-knit sweater dress I made you buy. Still, it's no reason to say I deserve death."

"I'm sorry," I say, reluctant to get into it. Especially since the words remain pressed behind my eyes, like a flashing neon sign that makes my head ache.

"PS," Kimmie continues, nodding toward my

sculpture of Adam's lips, "the assignment was to sculpt something *exotic*, not *erotic*. Are you sure you weren't so busy wishing me dead that you just didn't hear right? Plus, if it was eroticism you were going for, how come there's no tongue wagging out of his mouth?"

"And what's so exotic about *your* piece?"

"Seriously, it doesn't get more exotic than leopard, particularly if that leopard is in the form of a swanky pair of kitten heels. . . . But I thought I'd start out small."

"Right," I say, looking at her oblong ball of clay with what appears to be four legs, a golf-ball-size head, and a long, skinny tail attached.

"And, from the looks of your sculpture," she continues, adjusting the lace bandanna in her pixie-cut dark hair, "I presume you're hankering for a Ben Burger right about now. The question *is*, will that burger come with a pickle on the side or between the buns?"

"You're so sick," I say, failing to mention that my sculpture isn't of Ben's mouth at all.

"Seriously? *You're* the one who's wishing me dead whilst fantasizing about your boyfriend's mouth. Tell me *that* doesn't rank high up on the sick-o-meter."

"I have to go," I say, throwing a plastic tarp over my work board.

"Should I be worried?"

"About what?"

"Acting manic and chanting about death?"

"I didn't chant."

"Are you kidding? For a second there I thought you

were singing the jingle to a commercial for roach killer: *'You deserve to die! You deserve to die! You deserve to die!'* "

"I have to go," I say again.

"Camelia, wait. You didn't answer my question."

But I don't turn back. Instead, I go up and tell Ms. Mazur I'm not feeling well and need to go to the nurse. Luckily, she doesn't argue. Even luckier is that I know just where to find Ben.

DESIRE. DANGER. DESTINY.